JOE COFFIN

SEASON ONE

EPISODE ONE

ONE

JOE COFFIN

SEASON ONE

EPISODE ONE

KEN PRESTON

contents

Episode One

99

Jacob Mills' best friend, Peter Marsden, had been begging him for months to break into No. 99 Forde Road with him. He said maybe they would find a dead body in there, or maybe they would meet a ghost, or get chased by a zombie.

None of these things particularly appealed to Jacob, but Peter kept on and on at him, wearing him down, bit by bit.

The dilapidated, Victorian house had been empty for as long as they could remember. Every morning, as they walked past it on their way to school, they'd tell each other stories about ghosts wandering through the deserted rooms and corridors, skeletal hands clawing at the banisters as they shuffled down the stairs, blood dripping from their empty eye sockets. That's how Jacob wanted it to stay, a house that they visited only in their imaginations.

The house had been constructed of odd angles and weird extensions. Over the years, sections of it seemed to have sunk slightly, giving the rambling, pointed structure an even more unsettling appearance. Dark windows of different shapes and sizes sat uncomfortably with one another, some of them so recessed under the eaves it was difficult to imagine how they could receive any natural light. Vines trailed all across the frontage, around the weathered window frames and over the front door. Even the tall, tottering chimney pots were being slowly strangled by long, green fingers. Jacob was half convinced that one day he would walk past, and the house would be gone, completely hidden by a mound of twisted greenery.

A set of wide, stone steps, chipped and discoloured from years of neglect, led up to the front door. The steps were guarded by two stone gargoyles, squatting on pillars, their fat lips set in permanent sneers, baring their teeth at anyone foolish enough to approach them.

Jacob could never imagine himself walking past those gargoyles, fearful that they would spring to life, and pounce on him, sinking their stone teeth into his stomach and ripping out his guts.

The two ten year olds lived a few streets away, in River View Gardens, a rundown housing estate, notorious for the number of jobless who lived there. The estate had been built seven years ago, its architects promising it to be a bold new experiment in mixed social housing. Now the bigger, more expensive houses, lay empty or occupied by squatters, whilst the smaller houses were rented out mostly to single mothers and the unemployed.

In all the time that Jacob had lived in River View Gardens, he had never found a river there, or anywhere nearby.

Jacob and his mother and father had moved into a tiny box of a house on the estate when he was three years old. When he was eight, his father came home drunk one afternoon, and flew into a rage over nothing, it seemed to Jacob. His father had picked up a plate and hurled it across the tiny kitchen, where it smashed against a wall. And then he had picked up another, and hurled that one, and another, and another. Jacob's mother had been washing up at the kitchen sink, and she stood there helpless with fear, soap suds dripping from her hands held up in front of her face.

When he had finished hurling plates and mugs, Tom started venting his fury at his wife. Jacob had hidden under the kitchen table, sick with fear and shame, and watched as his father punched and slapped his mother around the head. When she fell to the floor, he began kicking her in the stomach.

Jacob had finally crawled out from beneath the table and rushed at his father, beating him on the back, and screaming at him to stop kicking his mother. Jacob's father had ignored him, probably hadn't even realised he was there, and only stopped when he heard the police pounding on the door, alerted by the call of a distressed neighbour.

The police found Jacob's father standing over his wife, his chest heaving as he sucked in great gulps of air, his fists clenched and his face contorted in anger. Jacob's mother lay curled up on the floor, tiny rivulets of blood running across the floor from beneath her head.

Jacob's father was arrested for assault. Jacob had only fragmented memories of that day, but he had gleaned enough knowledge over the years to work out what happened.

Jacob's mother refused to press charges, but the police prosecuted anyway. Jacob wondered why they bothered. They knew his father was part of the Slaughterhouse Mob, and sure enough, Mortimer Craggs supplied the best lawyers money could afford, and Jacob's father walked free.

Jacob had never thought his mum would take him back in again, but she did. He soon realised she couldn't afford not to. Jacob's father spent the next few months creeping around the house, trying to ingratiate himself with his wife and son. Jacob wondered what was going on, until he heard his mother talking to Steffanie one night, telling her how Craggs had leaned on Jacob's father, told him to keep his temper in check from now on. Said if anything like this happened again, Craggs would let Joe Coffin loose on him.

There was no mistaking what that meant.

Jacob was scared of his father, and greeted his awkward attempts at befriending him with sullen, monosyllabic replies. It was only a matter of a few days before the father gave up trying to make peace with his son, and they managed to exist in the same house without talking to one another, and by keeping out of each other's way.

Peter lived at the other end of the estate, in a house pretty much identical to Jacob's. Peter's mother always had a cigarette dangling from her mouth, or held between two fingers. When she finished one, she immediately lit up a second. Even outside, playing, if Jacob got close enough to Peter, he could smell the stale cigarette smoke on his clothes, and in his hair. Jacob once heard his mother and her neighbour, Doris, talking about Peter's mother. Doris said she was a slut, and Jacob's mother agreed. Jacob wasn't entirely sure what a slut was, but he knew it wasn't a nice term. He thought about telling Peter, but decided against it.

Both boys were small for their age, but the similarity ended there. Peter was thickset and bullish, like his mother. Jacob was slim built, and much quieter.

Peter had already explored the overgrown grounds of No. 99 with his best friend, Dougie. They had found a cellar door at the rear of the house, which had probably once been used for coal deliveries. The wood of the door was rotten, and Peter had been able to pull soft chunks of it free with his fingers, surprised woodlice scuttling over his hands and dropping to the ground.

The two friends had hatched a plan to break into the house, one day in the summer holidays. The trapdoor was padlocked, but the clasp was loose in the rotten wood. Peter said they could easily wrench it free. But then Dougie's family had moved away quite suddenly, and Peter had no desire to go exploring the rambling old house by himself.

Who knew what grisly horrors might confront him, once inside, and alone.

So he started working on Jacob, telling him the house was surely deserted, had been for years, and there was nothing to worry about, Peter would look after him. Jacob was reluctant, and took some persuading. It was autumn, the leaves turning brown and falling from the trees, before Peter convinced him that breaking into No. 99 was a good idea.

One Saturday afternoon, whilst Jacob's mother was out at work in the local supermarket, and Peter's mother was 'entertaining' a man friend in her bedroom, the two boys climbed over a fence at the rear of the house and dropped into the long, brown grass of No. 99. The sky was overcast and the light dull. Already, at two o'clock in the afternoon, it seemed as though night was creeping up on them.

Jacob's insides were loose with excitement and nerves. The boys crouched beside an enormous Ash tree, its dying leaves making a dry, rustling sound in the light breeze. They stared at the house, at its murky windows, their filthy net curtains already conjuring up images of ghosts in Jacob's head. Part of him wanted to run, and yet the windows, like monstrous eyes, captivated Jacob, and challenged him to venture inside and discover the house's secrets.

The two boys crept closer, until they were near enough that they could see the vague, shadowy shapes of furniture through the patio windows.

"I'm not sure I want to do this," Jacob whispered.

"Don't be a pussy!" hissed Peter. "You'd better come into that house with me, or I'm telling everyone at school that you're a queer!"

Jacob knew it was no idle threat. He followed Peter through the long grass and stingers, holding his hands up by his chest so that he wouldn't get stung, and approached the cellar door.

The clasp had been wrenched from the rotten wood, and it lay beside the trap door, the padlock still attached to it.

The two boys looked at each other.

"Did you do this?" Jacob said.

Peter shook his head. For once he seemed to have nothing to say.

Peter bent down and lifted the door open, propping it against the wall.

Jacob looked nervously at the stone steps disappearing into the gloom. He could hear the traffic rumbling along Forde Road, and some young kids playing hopscotch in a nearby street. Outside the grounds of No. 99, life was moving on as normal. But here, time seemed to have stopped. Even the leaves had stopped rustling in the wind, and there was no sign of the rats that the residents of the estate backing onto No. 99 complained of so often.

"Let's do it, then, yeah?" Peter said, his voice small and insubstantial, not his usual brash tone.

The two boys pulled torches out of their pockets and shone them down into the cellar. Thick strands of dusty cobwebs clung to the dank stone walls, and Jacob's torch light caught the movement of startled spiders, scurrying into gaps between the stonework.

Peter stepped carefully through the cellar opening first. He hesitated on the top step and turned, his eyes round and wide, to look at Jacob. As though perhaps willing his friend to call the whole thing off, and Peter wouldn't call Jacob a faggot, or tell anybody at school about their cowardice. The look only lasted a moment, before Peter began walking down the steps. As small as he was, he had to duck his head as he descended.

Jacob watched his friend disappearing into the dark. He thought about turning and running, leaving Peter to face whatever was in the house, alone. He could sprint back and climb over the garden fence, and be back in the safety of his own house in no time. Even the thought of having to endure Peter's taunts of 'Faggot!' and 'Pussy!' on Monday morning, didn't seem too bad right at that moment.

He had endured worse over the years.

But something in the darkness of that house called to him. The mystery that lay behind those blank windows appealed to him, in some grotesque, twisted way.

He stepped through the cellar opening, and followed his friend, descending into the black underbelly of the house.

Rivulets of dark, oily water trickled down the uneven cellar walls. As Jacob walked slowly through the cellar, he realised his feet were getting wet. He pointed his torch at the floor.

"Peter!" he whispered. "Watch out for all the puddles."

"How did all this water get in here?" Peter said. His voice wavered in the dark. He didn't sound anywhere near as confident as he had when he first talked about breaking in to No. 99.

"I think it must be seeping up through the floor." Jacob bent down and touched what he thought was a dry patch of ground. His fingers came away damp and dirty.

"Look at that, somebody's been digging a hole down here!" Peter pointed his torch at a large, dark shadow on the cellar floor.

Jacob approached it, shining his torch in the same direction. The hole was about six foot deep, and long and wide enough that it looked like a grave. There was an empty wooden box inside, like a coffin. The wood was stained a dirty, dark brown.

Beside the hole lay a sledge hammer and a spade, and a mound of black earth.

Behind the hole, in the further reaches of the cellar, was a collection of ancient, stone jars. They were scattered haphazardly over the floor, their lids by their sides.

Peter swung his torch around. "Bloody hell, look at that!"

Illuminated in the diffuse circle of torchlight, Jacob saw a pair of rusted jaws sitting on the floor, their teeth snapped shut, and pointing up to the ceiling. The two boys approached it with care, fearful that the jaws might open up, and snap their legs off.

"What is it?" Peter whispered.

"I think it's a mantrap," Jacob whispered back. "They were used for catching poachers a long time ago. If you step into it, it springs shut, and cuts off your foot."

"How do you know?" Peter said, scornfully.

Jacob shrugged. "I dunno. I think I heard about it in a history lesson, or something."

"Look over there, I bet that leads into the house."

In the pale light, Jacob could see a set of narrow steps disappearing up into the gloom. Stepping carefully past the large hole in the ground, Jacob and his friend walked slowly over to the bottom of the steps. They pointed their torches up, the combined light cutting through the darkness to reveal a closed wooden door at the top.

The two boys looked at each other.

"What do you think?" Peter whispered.

Jacob knew that his friend had lost all his bluster and confidence. At that moment, he could have said that he wanted to go back, and he knew

Peter would agree. There would be no name calling at school, no taunts of 'Faggot!' That Peter had not had the guts to explore the house, either, would be a secret to be kept forever, a bond between them as powerful as if they had.

This was Jacob's moment, when he could back out of their plan with no shame.

But his friend's bluster and name calling outside, had stung Jacob. A perverse desire for revenge festered in his mind.

"I think we should stick to the plan," Jacob said. "You're not scared, are you?"

"'Course not," Peter hissed. "I'm not a bloody queer, you know."

Peter took the steps first. Jacob regretted riling his friend, and losing his last chance to back out without losing face. Whatever happened next, he was sure Peter would insist on exploring the entire house.

"Come and help me," Peter said, pushing at the door.

Jacob joined him on the top step and the two boys pushed their shoulders against the old, heavy door, and shoved. It gave a little, and then some more, in tiny, juddering increments. The bottom edge of the door scraped against the floor, leaving curved trails of filth in its wake.

Once they had created a big enough gap, they slipped through, and into a narrow passageway. The floor was made up of uneven slabs of stone, and the walls whitewashed brick. After all the noise they had made, as they had forced the door open, the silence was shocking and oppressive.

On their left was a second door. Jacob peered through the dirty glass panes.

"This leads back outside," he whispered, hoping his friend would suggest that they use it and escape.

"There's another door down there," Peter said, pointing with his torch. "Let's see where it goes."

They crept down the passage, and Peter pushed open the door. They entered a large kitchen. The torch light rambled across wooden counter tops filled with broken plates and bowls, scattered silverware, and mounds of what looked like black ash. In the middle of the kitchen there was a massive, heavy table.

Jacob's torchlight strayed across the table, its surface dark with stains.

Jacob stared at the table like it was something completely alien to him. His lips had gone dry, and his tongue suddenly seemed too big for his mouth.

Jacob pointed his torch up. Hanging from the high ceiling, above the table, were rows of meat hooks. He shuddered a little, at the sight of them.

The two boys left the kitchen, and walked down the narrow passage and through another door. Now they were in the reception hall. In the silence of the house, Jacob could hear a lorry thundering by on the main road. But it sounded distant, as though the lorry was on the other side of town, or an echo from a different time.

In the weak light struggling through the filthy windows, they could see a broad staircase sweeping up to a galleried landing.

"Let's have a look upstairs," Peter whispered.

All Jacob wanted to do was make a run for it out of the front door.

He followed Peter up the stairs.

There were several doors on the landing, all closed apart from one, at the rear of the house. It was open just a crack, and Peter headed straight for it. Jacob could see the beam of his torch shaking as he walked.

It was no surprise when he heard Peter whisper, "Let's just look in here and then get out, yeah?"

"Yeah, I've got to get back," Jacob said.

"Me too," Peter replied. "Mum will be wondering where I am."

They were both lying, and they both knew it. It didn't matter anymore. They had crossed a threshold together, and neither one of them would grass on the other one for being scared.

Peter pushed at the door, and it opened easily and silently. Jacob was standing right behind him. Heavy curtains, hanging over the window, blocked out the last of the daylight. There was a big, old wardrobe standing in the corner, and a chest of drawers with ornate handles. Fat church candles sputtered and flared, puddles of wax gathering around them, where they sat on the floor. Greasy, black smoke curved upwards from the orange flames.

Jacob and Peter stood in silent terror, watching the man and woman on the bed in the flickering light of the candles. They were naked, the man lying on his back, his cock swollen and stiff. The woman was straddled across his chest. Both her hands were wrapped around his head, and she was thrusting her hips against his face, buried in her groin.

Her flame red hair cascaded in curls over her shoulders and down her back as she arched her head, her mouth open, as though she was about to scream.

Peter dropped his torch. It landed with a dull thud on the carpet.

The woman snapped her head around, tendrils of her hair falling across her face. She stared at the boys as she continued gyrating her hips against the man beneath her, pinning his head between her legs. His hands were on her buttocks, his fingers digging deep into her flesh.

The woman stared at Jacob, smiling slyly as she rocked back and forth. Jacob felt as though he was retreating deeper and deeper into his own mind, searching out the recesses and the hidden places, somewhere he could hide from this hypnotic, terrifying spectacle. But whatever he tried, her eyes followed him, penetrating into his most secret places and laying them bare.

A pink, pointed tongue flitted out of the woman's mouth, and she licked her upper lip, all the while still staring at the boys.

Peter screamed.

The spell was broken. Shocked out of their torpor, the two boys turned to run. Peter tripped and stumbled against the door, and it slammed shut. Jacob grabbed the handle, but the door wouldn't move, as though it was now part of the wall, as though it had never been opened at all.

Jacob heard movement behind them. Peter had already turned around, putting his back against the door. His eyes were wide and round, tears brimming over his lower lids, and he was mouthing words that Jacob could not hear.

He turned around. The woman had climbed off the bed. She was staring at them as she walked towards them, her movements slow and languid, like she had all the time in the world.

Her red curls, flowing over her shoulders, and the red triangle of hair between her legs, were a shocking contrast to her white, unblemished skin.

As was the dark red blood, running down the insides of her thighs.

Peter was sobbing, his face a blotchy mess of tears and snot. Jacob pushed at the door again, but still it refused to budge. The woman slowly licked her top lip again as she drew closer. Hoarse, throaty laughter filled the room. In the candle light, shadows flickered over the walls, seeming to dance along with the mad cackling.

Like a lithe cat suddenly tiring of its game, the woman pounced on Peter. She dragged him to the floor, straddling him like she had the man on the bed. Peter screamed, pounding at her naked chest, sobbing helplessly. The woman gazed at him, her tongue running along her top lip.

She grabbed his hair and yanked his head back, exposing the soft flesh of his throat.

Jacob looked away as she fastened her teeth on his friend's neck. Jacob wished he could block out the other boy's sobs, the sound of teeth tearing at flesh, and then he flinched as heard something snap, and Peter's screams turned into a wet gurgling and sucking gasp.

When Jacob looked back, he saw the naked man sitting up on the bed. His lips and teeth were smeared with the woman's blood, and it dribbled from his mouth, as he watched the woman huddled over Peter's limp body.

Jacob, realising he had been pushing at the door, pulled instead, and yanked it open. He tumbled outside, and sprawled across the landing. As he scrambled to his feet, he glanced back and saw through the open door the woman feeding on his friend, sucking at the wound in his throat. The man was crouched beside the woman, lapping like a dog at a gathering pool of blood on the floor.

Jacob ran for the stairs, his legs trembling and threatening to fold up beneath him with every step. Half running, half falling, he made it to the ground floor and ran for the cellar. The light was fading fast now, and he had left his torch upstairs where he had dropped it in his terror.

He stumbled down the passage, not daring to look back, even for an instant, and plunged headlong into the pitch black of the cellar. His feet slipped on the steps and he began falling out of control. His shoulder hit the stairs midway down, and then his head cracked against a step as he tumbled to the cellar floor.

Struggling to his feet, Jacob blinked warm blood out of his eyes. His hands were dripping with mud where they had landed in a puddle, and his head felt like someone had plunged a knife into it. But, even in his pain and terror, a small, rational part of his mind warned him to be careful of the large hole in the ground, and the mantrap.

Holding his hands out in front, Jacob shuffled cautiously forward in the dark.

Up ahead he saw a faint glow of grey against the total dark of the cellar. It was the open cellar door, leading outside, to freedom. Forcing himself to walk slowly and carefully, he headed for it. Once outside he could dash through the overgrown garden and leap over the fence, and then he would be safe. The first house he got to, he was going to pound on the door, beg for help. Maybe Peter was still alive, maybe it wasn't too late if the police came now.

Jacob got to the trap door and scrambled up the steps and into the garden. In the late afternoon darkness, he could just about pick out the massive Ash tree, and the fence behind it.

Stumbling towards freedom, long tendrils of grass grasping at his ankles, Jacob struggled not to burst into tears. If he started crying now, he knew he would collapse, and the monsters inside the house would have him.

He paused by the tree, leaning against the trunk, and steeled himself for the run across the last few yards, and then the scramble over the fence. He took several deep breaths, trying to calm himself.

A sudden blow from behind shoved him face down on the ground. Before he could scream, he had been flipped over on his back and a bloody hand clamped over his mouth. The woman's long tendrils of hair tickled his face as she leaned over him. Her mouth was smeared with blood.

Jacob tried biting her hand, struggling beneath her weight, but it was no good.

She leaned closer, her tongue slithering out of her sticky mouth, strings of red saliva hanging from her sharp teeth.

The terrified boy snapped his eyes shut, waiting for the sharp bite of her teeth in his neck.

skinny kids with tattoos

Joe Coffin looked at the tower block through the rain spotted windscreen. The car's suspension groaned a little as he shifted his bulk, trying to find a comfortable position. He hated riding in Tom's car, his head pressed against the roof, despite his best efforts to slouch in the seat. But then there was no room for his legs, either. He'd racked the seat back as far as it would go, but his knees were still up under his chin.

It was a big joke amongst the guys. Coffin didn't drive, never had. That was because, from about the age of eighteen, he'd grown too big to comfortably fit in most cars. It wasn't just his height, but his build, too. The others, they called him 'King Kong', or sometimes just 'Kong', but never to his face.

You didn't joke around calling Joe Coffin names. Not if you knew what was good for you.

Coffin was all muscle, looked like he'd been popping steroids all his life, and benchpressed car engines before breakfast. But it hadn't always been that way. When Coffin was a kid, he had been a tall, gangly piece of string. His father had owned a gym, was pretty big himself, and it seemed to Coffin that he was a source of shame to his father that he hadn't been born looking like a pro wrestler.

The gym wasn't one of those fancy places you get nowadays, all crappy pop music and water fountains and exercise machines. This was a scuzzy, sweaty gym, in that part of town you wouldn't visit unless you absolutely had to. You walked in Jim's gym, you'd better be ready to do some serious lifting. The membership was exclusively male, all huge, shaven headed, tattooed guys, with biceps thicker than a pretty girl's waistline.

That's where Joe Coffin had grown up, training with his dad, sparring with the other guys in the boxing ring, them all laughing at this scrawny, skinny kid, who was taller than some of his teachers at school, never mind the other kids in the class. He'd try and throw punches at them, or lift a puny little dumbbell, his face burning with shame, while the men sniggered, and humiliated him with their stupid taunts.

Looking back, he supposed he'd been trying to prove something to his father, trying to be the man he expected. Not that Coffin's father ever paid that much attention to him. Except sometimes with his fists.

But when he was sixteen, Coffin started packing on the muscle, and by the time he was eighteen, nobody was laughing at him anymore. Especially not the guys at the gym.

Tom Mills wiped furiously at the windscreen with an oily rag, replacing the mist from their breath with smeared streaks of grease and muck. In contrast to Coffin, Tom was small and wiry. He appeared to be older than his thirty-seven years, his skin flaky and blotchy, and his pinched cheeks making him look as though he was constantly sucking on a lemon.

"You ready?" Tom said.

"You sure this is the place?" Coffin said, still staring up at the tower block.

"Yeah, I told you, these are the guys." Tom stuck a cigarette in his mouth, struck a match against the zipper on his boot, and lit up.

"You sure?" Coffin said.

"Fuck, Joe, yeah I'm sure. One thousand and fucking ten percent sure, all right?"

Tom held out the open packet of cigarettes, and Coffin took one.

Tom lit it for him.

The cigarette smoke wafted across Coffin's field of vision. The tip tap of raindrops against the car roof started up again, rivulets of water running down the windscreen. Coffin watched as a young girl pushing a pram hurried past, her head down. Even inside the car he could hear the child screaming.

This was no place to bring up a kid.

"Tell me again, about these guys," Coffin growled.

Tom sighed, the smoke streaming from his mouth. "Come on, Joe, how many times do you want to hear this shit?"

"Quit whining, and tell me about them again."

"Okay, okay, like I said, these two guys, Shank and Ratface, they're metalheads, into this crazy vampire cult, called Midnight Deathskulls. They've got a little secret society going, like the Famous Five, or the Secret

Seven, only instead of getting into jolly scrapes and drinking ginger beer, they get together every night, and snort shit, tattoo each other, and fuck each other's brains out. Who knows, maybe the guys suck each other's dicks too. Whatever, like, you know, I'm a live and let live kind of guy, right? They can do whatever the fuck they want as long as they don't do it in front of me. But these two guys, Ratshank and Fuckface, or whatever the hell they're called, they think they're a pair of fucking vampires."

"Vampires."

"Yeah, I mean, what the fuck, right? I've seen them in town, wandering around wearing their pissy Goth clothes, faces covered in tattoos. And their teeth, man, they fucking file their teeth to points."

Coffin shifted uncomfortably in the car seat. His clothes, still smelling of prison starch, and stiff like cardboard, rustled as he moved. He'd got out of prison half an hour ago, picked up by Tom, and driven straight here. Six months for assault, let out early due to 'extenuating circumstances', and now, less than an hour into his freedom, and he was about to commit a much worse crime than the one he'd served time for.

Didn't matter to Coffin. This wouldn't be the first time he'd killed anyone.

"And they're the ones murdered Steffanie and Michael."

"Yeah," Tom said. "Best we can figure, they broke into your house to steal money for drugs. They were already high, and when they saw Steffanie and Michael, they lost it. Ripped their fucking throats out, with their teeth. Shit, man, they drank their fucking blood."

Coffin flinched. He stared at the tower block.

Vampires.

They liked to pretend.

Shit.

Coffin opened the door and climbed out of the car, the suspension creaking and groaning in protest. Tom followed him, locking the car and hurrying to catch up. They walked across a muddy patch of grass, pathetically labelled Play Area. It contained a single rusty swing, and a small slide.

Coffin was wearing his scuffed leather jacket over a sleeveless, white T-shirt. Rainwater ran down his close cropped scalp, and down the back of his neck. In his right hand he carried a cosh, made of a leather handle and a large, lead weight.

Entering the tower block, Coffin took one last drag on his cigarette and flicked it away.

They climbed the dingy concrete stairs, the walls damp with rainwater and the windows grey with dirt.

Tom wrinkled his nose. "Fucking hell, man, it stinks like a fucking blocked toilet in here. Some people are just filthy animals."

Coffin walked up the stairs without a word. When they reached the fifth floor, Coffin pushed open a door and they stepped into a dimly lit hall. Out of the six fluorescent strip lights spaced along the ceiling, only two were working, and one of those was flickering and buzzing, like it might give up at any moment.

As the two men walked down the hall, looking for apartment 5F, they could hear the muffled, rhythmic thud of heavy rock music. Coffin passed under the buzzing strip light, and the flickering, yellow glow gave his battered face a hellish appearance.

Coffin stopped outside 5F. The savage, relentless scream of thrash metal was so loud now, that when Coffin placed the flat of his hand against the door, he could feel the vibrations travelling up his arm. Tom stood behind Coffin, waiting for the signal that they were going in.

Two apartments down the hall, a door opened, and a young boy stuck his head out. He looked curiously at Coffin, his eyes growing wide at the sight of this huge beast filling the hallway. The boy's mother stepped outside, saw Coffin, and immediately dragged her child back inside, slamming the door behind her.

Coffin raised a heavily booted foot, and smashed the thin wooden door inwards. He stepped inside, swinging the cosh round and round. Tom stood in the doorway, blocking the exit. The room was filthy, littered with empty beer cans, cheap whisky bottles, and cardboard pizza trays, with mouldy, half eaten pizzas in them. Crude drawings of vampires had been scrawled across the walls in black, their pointed fangs impossibly large. Satanic symbols had been drawn in the spaces between the vampires.

In the far corner a bare chested man sat on the floor, his braided hair hanging lankly over his scrawny shoulders, his head lolling forwards on his chest. Across from him, set between two of the biggest speakers that Coffin had ever seen, was a record player, the black vinyl disk spinning round and round.

In the middle of the room, a man lay on top of a woman, on a bare, filthy mattress. They were both naked, and she was raking her fingers down his back, and chewing on his neck, her other hand clutching his skinny backside as it pumped frantically up and down.

None of them noticed that they had visitors.

Coffin walked over to the record player and kicked it over, the music cut dead with sharp squawk. The sudden silence was like a bucket of cold water in the face, after the unrelenting noise of the savage music.

The naked white kid, his pasty flesh covered in badly inked tattoos, scrambled to his feet. The woman lying on the stained mattress yanked at a threadbare sheet to cover herself. Coffin noticed her teeth, badly filed to sharp, ugly points.

"What the fuck?" the kid yelled, his outraged voice cutting through the silence. His hands were clenched into fists. His neck looked okay, where the girl had been biting him. A few scratches, but she hadn't drawn much blood.

Just as Tom had said. They liked to pretend.

"Get out," Coffin snarled at the woman.

She grabbed her pile of clothes and ran for the door, still naked. She stopped when she reached Tom, standing in the doorway, blocking her exit. He smirked at her, before stepping aside to let her out, and smacked her on the arse as she scooted past him.

"Hey, man, I paid good money for her," the kid yelled, spittle flying from his lips. "The fuck you think you doin?"

Coffin strode up to the kid, towering over him, and smashed the cosh into his nose. The kid howled, blood exploding from his ruined nose, and staggered back a step. The other kid looked up, a flicker of interest passing over his stupefied face, before his chin dropped back onto his chest.

The pasty white boy fell to the mattress, holding his nose, blood dribbling between his fingers. He reached under the mattress, and pulled out a gun. Coffin kicked the gun out of his hand, and then stomped on his chest. The kid screamed, blood and spittle spraying from his mouth.

Coffin rolled him over onto his front, grabbed his wrist and twisted his arm up behind his back until he heard a snap. The kid screamed again, and started sobbing.

Coffin picked up the gun and pressed the muzzle against the back of the kid's shaved skull.

"You like to pretend being vampires, right?" Coffin said, his voice low.

"That's what I've heard. You like drinking blood."

"No, please!"

Coffin jammed the muzzle of the gun into the back of the kid's head. He screamed.

"Tell me," Coffin said. "Tell me that you like pretending to be vampires. Tell me about the blood."

The kid hung his head, snot and blood hanging in a long, thick string from his broken nose.

"Fuck, Joe, just shoot the bastard," Tom said.

Coffin bent down, his mouth next to the kid's ear.

"Tell me about it," he whispered. "Tell me how you like getting high, and drinking other people's blood."

The kid nodded his head, still sobbing.

"Joe, come on!" Tom hissed, walking further into the bare room. "If I'd known you wanted to fucking interrogate the little piece of shit, we could have taken him back to the club. We haven't got time!"

Coffin looked up at Tom, stared at him for a long second. Then, his mind made up, he turned back.

"This is for Steffanie and Michael, you sick bastard," Coffin snarled.

"What?" he sobbed. "What are you talking abou—"

Coffin pulled the trigger, spraying the kid's brains over an empty pizza box. He let go of his arm, and the body hit the floor with a solid thump, the kid's face smacking into the bloody mess on the pizza box.

"What about him?" Tom said, pointing at the other one, who looked like he had passed out.

Coffin walked over, and shot him in the chest, pulling the trigger repeatedly until it just clicked, and the kid's chest looked like a slab of bloody meat.

Coffin dropped the gun on the floor. "Let's get out of here."

Tom stepped aside to let Coffin out, who had to duck as he stepped through the doorway. Tom pulled out a handkerchief and wiped the gun clean of prints. He took one last look around, and his gaze settled on the record deck, lying upside down, the sound system and the huge speakers.

"Who the fuck buys records anymore?" he muttered.

Then he followed Coffin outside.

* * *

Coffin spent the rest of the afternoon getting drunk, in the tiny flat above the Blockade. He heard Lucy, the barmaid, opening up, putting a tune on the jukebox. Some crappy pop song by a faceless group of teenagers with long hair and pimples, no doubt.

Coffin stayed upstairs, sitting on the settee, his enormous bulk making it look ridiculously tiny. He swigged whisky from a bottle, and when he had drained it, he searched the kitchen for another, sweeping the tins of vegetables and stew aside until he found what he was looking for. He cracked open the seal, and upended the bottle, swallowing great gulps of whisky, hoping to lose himself, to obliterate his memories and every last trace of his life.

Today he had done what he set out to achieve, two months ago, after the murder of his wife and son. He had found their killers, and executed them, as they deserved.

Why then did he still feel so bad? So empty of anything resembling humanity? Coffin had killed before, and done a great many other bad things, too. So why, today, did he feel as though he had crossed a threshold? Stepped beyond even his unfocused moral code?

Coffin took another swig from the bottle. The little shits deserved it. Forget how young they looked, how pathetic, their brains peppered with holes from all the shit they snorted. They were killers.

They deserved to die.

Coffin had first seen Steffanie dancing at the nightclub, Angellicit. The club was owned by Terry Wu, who was paying protection money to Craggs. Rumour had it that Wu had been a notorious Triad gangster in China, and that his role as owner of Angellicit was simply cover for a drug smuggling ring.

Coffin never saw any evidence of that on his rounds.

Terry Wu was a round blob of a man, squeezed into an expensive suit. His face was always shiny with sweat, and he was constantly mopping his forehead with a silk handkerchief. He smiled and laughed a lot, clapped you on the back like you were his best friend, said the drinks were on the house.

Coffin was never easy in Wu's company. He knew you couldn't trust a man like that, who tried so hard to be your friend all the time.

Coffin had been out collecting payments. Craggs said he wouldn't always be doing that, being the muscle, the tough guy. Craggs said he had big plans for Joe Coffin, plans for a partnership. And then, when Craggs retired, Coffin would be the leader of the Slaughterhouse Mob.

"Playing at being a tough guy, that's for the gorillas," Craggs once said. "They like to use their fists and their feet, see how much damage they can do. But you know what, Joe? I worked something out a long time ago. Men like that, it's all about their manhood, know what I'm saying? Stead of beating the crap out of some poor sod, they should get together and get their dicks out, compare sizes. That's all it is to them, who's got the biggest dick. It's kinda queer, when you think about it. All these big, tough gorillas, making a lot of noise and pounding their chests, beating up the fairies for fun, when all the time, deep down inside, they're just faggots themselves. But you, Joe, you're better than that."

So Coffin did the rounds, collecting the payments. The scuzzy lowlifes who ran the bars, and the clubs, and the massage joints, Coffin was happy to take money from them. After all, they were in the business, they already knew that the protection racket was part of the deal, something to be put up with. But it was the smaller businesses, the newsagents, the corner shops, run by families struggling to stay afloat, Coffin felt bad about taking their money. Sometimes he only took half of what they were supposed to pay. Before he got back, he would redistribute the cash, so that the lowlifes took the blame for the underpayments.

There was payback, and they protested, but it did no good. Coffin knew they thought he was pocketing the money himself, but that didn't bother him. No one was going to grass Joe Coffin up.

It was well known in the clubs and bars in Birmingham that Joe Coffin was like a son to Mortimer Craggs. And although Craggs was an old man now, his reputation was still powerful enough that everybody who knew of him lived in fear of him.

So, Coffin had been out, and he collected his money from Wu, and decided to stay for a drink, check out the talent. Steffanie stood out from the other dancers. Sure, she had the long legs, smooth, tanned body, and the fiery, curly hair. But she also had a poise, and a look in her eyes, a defiance, an independence, which turned Coffin on.

Six months later, and they were married in a registry office, just the two of them and the registrar, and some poor guy they dragged in off the street as a witness. When they'd finished, Coffin stuffed a fistful of bills into his hand, and told him to get lost.

Five months after that and Michael was born. And when big, tough, Joe Coffin cradled his new born son in his arms, he cried.

Coffin stood up, letting the whisky bottle drop to the floor, where it rolled across the carpet. He walked into the kitchen and turned on a tap, splashing the cold water against his face.

Now that Coffin had exacted his cold revenge, what else did he have to live for?

Drying his face on a rough, scratchy towel, Coffin heard a light knocking at the door.

He walked through the flat, kicking an empty bottle out of the way, sending it spinning across the carpet. He opened the door.

Laura Mills stood framed in the doorway, skinny arms pale like she never saw the sun, hands clasped in front of her mouth. Her lank, dirty blond hair framed her thin face and red rimmed eyes.

"Hi Joe."

Coffin said nothing. The whisky was making it difficult for him to think.

"Joe?" Laura said, in her tiny, vulnerable voice. "Can I come in?"

"Sure." Coffin stepped out of the way, let her walk through the doorway.

He closed the door, watched her as she picked up the empty whisky bottle. She turned and looked at him, and he saw his own agonising pain reflected in her face. She walked in the kitchen, placed the bottle on the counter.

"What do you want, Laura?" Coffin growled.

She turned around, stared at him, her eyes round, like she was suddenly scared of him.

"I'm sorry, Joe," she said.

"Yeah? What for?"

"I'm sorry about Steffanie, and Michael."

"You already said that, at the funeral."

"I know."

Coffin nodded, and went and sat down on the couch. Laura was still in the kitchen, and he couldn't see her anymore. But then she appeared at the doorway, leaned against the door frame. He clenched and unclenched his hands, trying to focus all his nervous energy into that single, repeated action.

Killing those two kids had meant to be cathartic, the rough justice giving him a sense of finality, revenge. But in truth, it had done the opposite.

Instead of sating his bloodlust, the killings had stirred the beast within, poking and prodding it in its cave. Coffin's need to mete out more violence coursed through his veins like lava, his head pounding with its desire.

"Joe?"

Coffin looked up.

Laura's eyes glistened, and a tear trickled down her cheek. She wiped at her eye, smudging her mascara, leaving a black smear across her face.

"Joe, I need you," Laura whispered.

Coffin hung his head, his thick arms resting on his legs, still clenching and unclenching his hands.

"I know this is an awful time for you, Joe, and I'm sorry I came here, I'm sorry to ask you this, but you're the only one I can turn to."

Coffin remained silent, focusing all his energy into his fists.

"Damn you, Joe!" Laura shouted, and stepped over to Coffin and punched him on the arm. "Don't you dare do this to me! Don't you dare ignore me!"

She was sobbing now, and she collapsed into the threadbare chair opposite Coffin, plunging her face into her hands, the muffled sobs growing louder.

Coffin got off the settee, knelt down in front of her, putting his arms around her and resting his forehead on her shoulder.

"What's wrong, Laura? Why are you here?"

"It's Jacob!" Laura gasped, each word punctuated with another sob. "He's gone missing, and I don't know what to do!"

gyms are for wimps

Emma Wylde took the stairs two at a time, her trainers slapping against the metal steps, the noise echoing around the stairwell. She swung around in a tight, right turn, and then up the next flight as fast as she could go. She shouldn't have been here, these were the fire escape stairs, but she didn't have anywhere else to do her hill training. Bloody city was too busy with commuters and shoppers crowding the pavements to get any serious running in. And she didn't have time in her lunch break to find somewhere she could run on the trails.

Emma knew she could have used the regular stairs, but then she would have had to dodge the office workers heading for their lunch break, or back to the office, put up with people staring, or colleagues laughing at her. Even today, in the age of the couch potato, when most people preferred taking the lift just one floor instead of walking, there were still far too many people on the stairs for Emma's liking.

Not only did she need the stairs for the strenuous exercise, but she needed her space to help clear her head. Emma wasn't a sociable person, happier with her own company than that of other people, which was ironic, considering she was a reporter.

She was puffing with the effort now, a sheen of sweat on her forehead. It was a cool day outside, the sky grey and overcast, threatening rain. Emma's blond hair was tied back in a short ponytail, and she was wearing shorts and a black T-shirt.

She reached the top, shouted, "Twenty-four!" and spun around on the spot, ready to descend. Ten floors, back down to the ground and then a last sprint back up to the tenth floor, making twenty-five sets in total. Emma checked her stopwatch as she set off.

She picked up her speed, dangerously close to losing her footing and tumbling down the stairs. But she had to keep moving, if she was going to beat her personal best. The windows and doors became a revolving blur as she dashed around the corners and then down another flight of steps. She hit the ground floor and immediately turned around and began the sprint back up the stairs.

Spikes of pain shot through her chest, her breath coming in short gasps, calf muscles burning. The echo of her shoes hitting the metal steps pounded through her brain, like the sound was coming from inside her head, not from her environment. She ignored the temptation to sneak a quick peek at her stopwatch, it would only slow her down. Just had to concentrate on the climb, get back to that tenth floor as quickly as possible.

As soon as Emma's feet stumbled onto the tenth floor landing, she hit the stop button on her watch. Sitting down on the floor, breathing hard, and blinking sweat out of her eyes, she stared at the digital display.

"Fuck, shit, fucking bastard!"

That was her third time now, unable to get near her personal best, let alone beat it. What the hell was wrong with her? Her times were getting worse, not better. Emma hung her head between her knees, watching beads of sweat drop from her forehead and land on the metal grill below.

Once her breathing had calmed down, Emma climbed unsteadily to her feet, and pushed open the fire escape door. She retrieved the folded piece of cardboard she had used to wedge the door open, so she wouldn't get locked out, and let it swing shut behind her. The silence of the fire escape stairs, where the only sounds had been her feet hitting the steps, her breath, and the thud of her blood rushing through her head, was suddenly replaced by the clatter and hubbub of the newsroom.

Row after row of desks and cubicles stretched across almost the entire top floor of the Metropolitan Tower. Large windows on three sides offered views across the city. Across the fourth wall were a row of large screen televisions, all tuned into different news stations, subtitles rolling across the bottom.

"Hey, Ems, nice sweat you got going there," called a voice from the chaos of the newsroom. "Anytime you wanna rub that sweaty body up against mine, just let me know!"

"Fuck you, Rick!" Emma shouted back, giving him the finger.

"Tell me where and when, I'll be there!" Rick shouted, leaning back in his chair and clasping his hands behind his head, a huge grin on his face. The man at the desk opposite stretched across, and they high-fived each other.

"Bloody hell, Emma, look at the state of you," Karl Edwards said, standing outside his office, arms folded over his round stomach. "I thought it was you I could hear, making all that noise."

Emma swiped her arm across her forehead, wiping the sweat away. "You ever think about wearing a bib, when you eat lunch, Karl?"

"Huh?"

Emma pointed. "Either you cut yourself shaving this morning, or you got ketchup on your tie."

"Oh shit." Karl pulled a handkerchief out of his pocket and began scrubbing at the red splodge.

"I thought Mrs Edwards had you on a diet? I swear to God I saw you eating a salad yesterday."

"Yeah, you saw right. I should've been eating salad today, but I chucked it in the bin when I got in this morning, and bought myself burger and chips." Karl scrubbed at his tie some more, but only succeeded in spreading the red splodge further out. "Hell's teeth, I'm going to have to buy myself a new tie now."

"It's worse than that, Karl," Emma said. "You're going to have to buy yourself the exact same tie, unless you want Mrs Edwards to find out you've been cheating on her with the burger van man."

"She's been nagging at me about my lifestyle for a while now," Karl said, spitting on his handkerchief and then scrubbing some more. "Says I need to cut down on my fats, drink less alcohol and coffee. Says she's concerned about my cholesterol, and my free radicals."

"Free radicals?" Emma said, grimacing as Karl spit into his handkerchief again.

"Don't ask me," Karl grunted. "I thought they were a pop group when she first mentioned them."

"I'm going to freshen up," Emma said.

"Soon as you're done, I want to see you in my office." Karl gave up on his tie, and yanked it from his collar.

"Okay, Boss." Emma began walking away.

"Hey, Emma," Karl said. "What do you do, go in the toilets and have a strip wash over the sink?"

"Yep." Emma kept walking.

"Well, that's not hygienic, you know? Besides which, the rest of us, we don't like it when you lock us out of the toilets while you're washing yourself down."

"If you put a shower in I could have a proper wash, and you and the rest of the monkeys around here could take a piss whenever you wanted."

"That right? You think we're made of money? Why do you have to do your training here, anyway? Why the hell can't you join a gym, like everybody else?"

"Gyms are for wimps," Emma called over her shoulder as she walked off, to catcalls and whistles.

* * *

After freshening up, and stowing her running gear in a gym bag, Emma met with Karl in his office. She wore trousers, shirt open at the collar, and a jacket. The men sometimes tried teasing her, said she looked more like a guy than they did. She said that wasn't possible, not without a beer gut.

Karl waved her in, and she sat down opposite him. A news report was playing, on a large screen television attached to the wall, but the sound was muted.

"Feel all better now?" Karl said. He was still tieless, his collar unbuttoned.

"Yep, fresh as a fucking daisy," Emma said. "What did you want?"

"Do you have to talk like that?" Karl said. "I mean, come on, would it hurt if sometimes you could try and act a bit more like a lady, and not swear all the time?"

"What is this, are we back in the 1950s all of a sudden? Next you'll be asking me to pop out to the shops and look for a replacement tie for you."

Karl opened his mouth, and then snapped it shut again.

"You fucking were, weren't you?" Emma shook her head. "Is that what you wanted to ask me? Because if it is, if you think I'm going to simper down to the shops, every time you dribble your food on your tie, I'm out of here now."

Karl held up his hand. "For crying out loud, just stop, will you?" He let his hand drop to the desk. "Remember that lead you were working on a while back? Steffanie Coffin?"

"Course I do." Emma sank back in her chair. She felt sick every time she thought of Steffanie, and her little boy Michael.

"You got that look on your face again," Karl said. "Like you're the one responsible for them getting killed."

"It still feels that way to me."

"Yeah, well, it shouldn't. Steffanie knew what she was doing, she knew the risks. You were offering her a way out of the life, Emma. That was a good thing you were doing for her."

"That's not the way it turned out, though. She came to me for help, and instead, I got her and her little boy killed." Emma leaned forward in her chair, and pointed at her editor. "I swear, Karl, that's what happened. Mortimer Craggs ordered a hit on her, because he found out she was passing me information about Terry Wu's murder."

"You don't know that, Emma," Karl said. "You're the only one thinks that way. You saw the stories on the news, and in the papers."

"Yeah," Emma said, her voice low. "The whole country thinks we got Count fucking Dracula prowling the streets. The only reason we haven't found him yet is because he stalks the city wearing his invisibility cape."

"You never read Dracula, did you, Emma?"

"He doesn't have an invisibility cape?"

"No. You're confusing him with Harry Potter."

"Well, fuck, Karl, maybe Dracula stopped off at Hogwarts on the way over here, and Harry loaned him his invisibility cloak. Because, you know what? That's just as credible a story as all the shit I read about those two murders."

"You still don't know Craggs had them killed. That thing with Terry Wu and Steffanie, could be a coincidence. You really think that Craggs would have had Steffanie and Michael sliced and diced like that? He would have ordered a hit on them, not a horror movie gore fest."

"Are you sure about that?" Emma said, sinking back into her chair. "I've heard some pretty graphic stuff from when Craggs was younger, from when he was making a name for himself and the Slaughterhouse Mob. You ever hear that story about the blow torch?"

"Emma—"

"Craggs used it to burn the lips off some poor bastard who'd been chatting up his wife in the pub he owned back then. She was the barmaid, I always thought flirting with the customers was part of the job description. Poor bastard had to have a skin graft from the nose down, and spent the rest of his life eating pureed food, and pissing his pants every time someone struck a match."

"Emma, you know none of those stories have ever been proved. Craggs hasn't even got a parking ticket to his name."

"Yeah, well, I'm telling you, Karl, we get Craggs for that murder, and he won't have to worry about parking tickets for the rest of his life. And with Craggs in jail, the whole gang folds. They're nothing without him."

"It's not going to happen, Emma," Karl said, softly. "Not yet, anyway."

"Yeah, I know. I wanted a career making story, and all I've got now is blood on my hands. I just hope Joe Coffin never finds out, because then I'm dead for sure."

"Yeah, well, Joe Coffin's sort of why I asked you in here, in the first place." Karl opened a drawer and pulled out a cigar. He stuck it in his mouth and began chewing on it.

Emma sat up again. "What are you talking about, Karl?"

"Remember those two boys went missing, a few days back?"

"Yeah, a couple of ten year olds, right? What were their names, um, Peter Marsden and . . .?"

"Jacob Mills. That name ring any bells with you?" Karl shifted the cigar from one side of his mouth to the other.

"Sweet fuck, you're telling me that Jacob is Tom Mills' kid?"

"That's right, and the coincidence doesn't stop there, because Tom Mills is married to Laura Mills, previously known as . . ."

"Laura Coffin." Emma snapped her fingers together. "Is Jacob, Joe Coffin's kid?"

"No, Joe and Laura divorced twelve years ago, so Jacob is Tom's kid, poor little bastard. With a piece of shit like Tom Mills for your father, he's got no chance."

"So, you think Jacob's disappearance has got something to do with Steffanie's murder?"

Karl took the unlit cigar out of his mouth. The end was all chewed and soggy, and Karl had to pull flakes of tobacco off his tongue before answering. "I don't know, to be honest, but it's a coincidence, and, despite what I said earlier, I don't like coincidences." He popped the cigar back in his mouth. "Pete's covering the story, but he phoned in sick today, so I wondered if you wanted to take it on, in his absence."

"Won't Pete mind?"

"I don't give a shit what Pete thinks. Last time he phoned in sick we didn't see him for two months, because he was on an almighty bender. I thought you could go and interview the kids' mothers, take Jonny with you, see if he can get some nice shots of them blubbing, something that'll look good on the front page tomorrow morning."

"You're all heart, Karl," Emma said, as she stood up.

"Hey, wait a sec," Karl said, pulled open his desk drawer, and produced his ketchup stained tie. "While you're out and about, if you happen to be passing a tie shop . . ."

Emma snatched the tie from him.

"I ought to fucking strangle you with it," she said, and stalked out of his office.

black and shiny

His wrists were red raw, and he had to clench his teeth to stop from crying out every time the rough rope chafed against his skin. The iron rung, bolted into the cellar wall, was old and rusty, and Jacob had spent the last few hours scraping the rope against it, hoping it would fray and split. He had to work quickly, ignore the pain, because the woman would be down to see him soon, with his food. She always untied him, and sat and watched him while he ate the thin soup, and the bread, with trembling hands.

When he had finished eating, then came the worst part, when she would unwrap the blood soaked cloth around his left arm, and re-open the wound. Jacob cried and screamed, and struggled and kicked, and tried to bite her, and sometimes he fainted from the pain. But however much he fought, the woman was always stronger than him, and she would bleed him, filling a small silver bowl with his dark red blood. And when she had enough, she always bound his arm back up again, and tenderly stroked his sweat covered brow, before leaving him alone once more.

Jacob was feeling weaker every day, so much so he sometimes passed out. Then he would wake up shivering and sick, leaning awkwardly against the damp wall, and wondering how long had passed since he had fainted.

But he knew he had to try and keep alert, stay strong. If she found him now, and untied him, she would see the frayed rope, she'd know he was trying to escape. Jacob closed his eyes, tears squeezing out between his eyelashes, and strained against the rope cutting into his wrists, forcing it up and down against the rusty edge of the iron bar.

His shoulders were sore, and his back ached. Sometimes his arms cramped up, and he cried with the pain. He had lost track of time, trapped in the dank, dark cellar. That first night, after they had dragged him down here and tied him up, the man had come back and spent the next couple of hours repairing the cellar door.

When the man had finished, Jacob heard him padlock it shut, plunging the ten year old boy into darkness. Jacob barely slept, shivering with cold and fear, uncomfortable and sore, sitting against the damp, rough brickwork. His mind was crazy with fear, alternately wondering why they had kept him alive, and thinking up dreadful tortures that awaited him.

Soon enough, the rustling and squeaking of rats scurrying through the cellar had added to his terror. They scrabbled across his feet, making him scream and kick out wildly, and once he woke up to the sensation of a rat gnawing through the sole of his trainer. He stamped and kicked in the darkness, and heard the rat squealing, and scampering away.

Sometimes, that first night, he wondered if Peter might be alive, too, and held captive somewhere else in the house. But then he remembered the woman attacking his friend, and all the blood spilling onto the faded carpet. He remembered the man lapping at the puddles of blood, like a thirsty dog.

Jacob kept scraping the rope against the iron rung. Fear that he would be found out before he had set himself free, kept him going. The pain in his wrists was nothing compared with the horror of what those monsters might do to him if they caught him trying to escape.

Both of his captors scared him, but the woman especially. Maybe that was because he knew her. She had been his mum's friend. Steffanie always brought Jacob a present when she came to visit, and Jacob had always enjoyed playing with her little boy, Michael.

But she should be dead.

At this thought, Jacob always felt as though his mind would tip over into a black pit of madness. Because he knew that Steffanie and Michael had been murdered. His mum had tried to hide the knowledge from him, tried telling him that they had died in a car accident, but Jacob knew the truth. He'd seen the newspaper headlines in the newsagents, and he'd heard his school friends talking about it.

Steffanie and Michael were dead. He had been to their funeral, seen their caskets lowered into the ground, whilst Joe Coffin fell to his knees and wept.

Joe had always scared Jacob. He was so big and powerful, that whenever he stood in front of Jacob, Joe seemed to blot out most of the sunshine. He came to their house in River View Gardens once, and stood in their tiny kitchen. He seemed to take up half the room, his head almost touching the ceiling. When he left, Jacob expected to see his footprints smashed into the floor, a spider web of cracks spreading out from each one.

But Joe had never hurt Jacob, or said anything mean to him. Not like Jacob's father. And seeing Joe at the funeral, so desolate with grief, he'd looked smaller and more helpless than Jacob could have ever imagined.

Jacob kept scraping at the rope. Steffanie was alive, but she wasn't the Steffanie that he used to know and like. This Steffanie was monstrous, she was evil. Jacob had tried pleading with her to set him free. He'd tried reminding her of who he was, and how kind she used to be with him.

But she paid him no notice. She fed him, and gave him water. And she opened up his wound and bled him.

The rope snapped and Jacob fell forward onto the floor, his face smacking into a puddle of dirty water. He tried to push himself up, but he was too weak, and his arms started to tingle with pins and needles. Jacob managed to rollover onto his back, and lay there flexing his fingers, trying to bring life back to his hands and arms.

Moisture seeped through the back of his shirt, chilling his back. Jacob wiped dirty water out of his eyes, his fingers numb and clumsy. He sat up as the pins and needles began to wear off, replaced in his left arm by a dull throb around the site of his festering wound. The pain was growing in intensity, and Jacob could smell the stink of infection.

Now that he was free of the rope he realised that it might all have been for nothing. The trapdoor leading outside, to the garden, was padlocked shut. Jacob hadn't given any thought to whether or not the inner door into the cellar would be locked too.

His eyes had grown used to the darkness, and Jacob could pick out a faint rectangular border of light, at the top of the cellar steps. He had no idea of the time. Was that daylight outside, or was it night time, and what he could see was light cast from a bulb, or candles?

Jacob shifted on to his knees. Gingerly placing the flat of his hand against a damp wall, he shakily climbed to his feet. A wave of nausea and dizziness washed over him, his vision greying out, and for a moment he was scared that he might faint. But it passed, and his vision returned.

Still leaning against the wall for support, Jacob shuffled over to the steps. He had worked so hard these last few hours, sawing through his bonds, he hadn't given much thought to what he would do next. And now he was free of the rope, all he wanted to do was sit and cry, and call for his mummy.

What would he do if, when he reached the top of the cellar steps, the door was locked? If he could only scream loud and long enough, perhaps he could alert a passer-by. He had tried screaming, the first few hours of his captivity, until his throat had grown sore and hoarse, and his cries for help were little more than a croak. But nobody had come, not even the Steffanie monster, or the man. The cellar was too far away from the road, around the back of the house. Nobody could hear him.

Jacob doubted that he could make himself heard more from the top of the steps than he could in the cellar. The big, old house was just too far away from the main road, heavy with traffic, drowning out any of his faint cries for help that might actually carry that far.

But if he could just get outside, down to the front of the drive, somebody would see him then. Somebody would rescue him.

Jacob took the first step, and then the next. He leaned against the wall, taking a deep, juddering breath of the cold air.

Gritting his teeth, he continued climbing the steps. Time was growing short, he was convinced of that. He had to get out, before he was discovered.

At the top of the steps, Jacob paused again to recover his strength. Struggling his way up that short flight of steps had felt like climbing a mountain. Taking another deep breath he leaned his shoulder against the door, twisted the handle, and pushed.

Nothing.

The door didn't budge.

It was locked.

Tears rolled down Jacob's filthy cheeks as a wave of despair washed over him, and he sank to his knees. He was trapped in this filthy cellar for the rest of his life, whilst the Steffanie monster bled him dry. Or until the infection in his arm killed him.

He wished he had never agreed to explore No. 99 with Peter. If only he had refused, if he had not been worried about Peter's schoolboy taunts, or if the cellar trapdoor had not been broken open already. Or if this door he was leaning against had been locked, they would have had to turn around and go back home.

And none of this nightmare would have happened, and Peter would still be alive, and Jacob wouldn't be trapped down here, slowly dying.

But the door hadn't been locked, had it? The two boys had struggled to open it, as it scraped against the flag stoned floor along the passageway outside, but it wasn't locked.

Jacob lifted his head.

It wasn't locked.

And every time Evil Steffanie came to feed him and bleed him, he heard the door scraping along the floor as she opened it.

Jacob stood up and braced his shoulder against the cracked wooden panel. He gathered his strength and pushed as hard as he could.

Noisily, it gave a little, and a chink of light fell on Jacob's face. He pushed again, and it gave a little more. It was too difficult. The last time he had pushed this door open, there had been two of them. And he had been healthy, and strong.

Jacob realised his wrists were bleeding, where the rope had scraped away the skin. He looked at the bandage on his arm. A fresh, dark patch of blood was seeping through the fabric, along with yellow pus, stinking of infection.

He had to get out of there. If he stayed in the cellar much longer he would die, even if the Steffanie monster did not kill him for trying to escape.

Jacob shoved his shoulder against the wooden door once more, a weak sliver of light falling across his face, taunting him with the possibility of freedom. He closed his eyes, clenched his jaw, and with a silent prayer to God, *please, please, let the door open this time,* he pushed as hard as he could.

The door scraped noisily open another inch, got caught on something, and then juddered open another inch or two, and stopped.

Jacob sank to the floor, gasping, his whole body trembling. He knelt on the floor, sweat dripping from his face, shivering in the cold, waiting for his heart to stop thumping so hard in his chest.

Waiting to find out if he had been discovered, with all the noise he had made opening the door.

Jacob raised his head and looked through the gap between the door and the door frame. He could see the stone flagged passage, illuminated by rays of weak, autumnal sunlight, struggling through the dirty panes of glass in the back door.

The door that led outside, to the garden at the rear of the house.

To freedom.

Jacob pressed his face against the gap, the edges of the door and the frame pressing into his cheeks.

He hadn't pushed the door open enough, the gap was too narrow for him to fit through. He stepped back and shifted position, thrusting his wounded arm through the gap first, and then his shoulder. That was as far as he could get.

Jacob screamed in frustration, and kicked at the door, and pounded at it with his free arm. Then he stopped, and held his breath.

Had he heard something? He strained to listen above the thumping of his heart, holding his breath for as long as he could. Finally he let his breath out in an explosive whoosh, and gasped for air.

Jacob pushed at the door again, his shoulder still jammed in the gap. But he had used the last of his fading strength to push it open this far. He had nothing left. If only it was another inch wider, he was sure he could squeeze through.

Jacob swallowed back the tears threatening to overwhelm him. He just had to keep pushing at the gap between the door and the frame. Surely he could force his way through if he kept pushing?

Then he heard the noise again. The slow shuffle of footsteps on the stone floor. The rustle of clothing.

Someone was coming.

Jacob tried pulling himself back through the doorway. But he was stuck. He had pushed so hard in his attempt to wriggle his way through the gap that he was now jammed halfway.

The shuffling footsteps drew closer, and Jacob could hear slow, ragged breathing, and grunting, as though the effort of walking was sheer torture.

Wide eyed, Jacob stared through the gap he had made, as a shambolic, hunched figure slouched into his line of view.

"Peter!" Jacob gasped.

The boy's delight, at seeing his friend alive, disappeared like a puff of smoke on a windy day.

Peter's throat had been ripped wide open, and Jacob could see the ropey muscles, glistening red, and flexing and contracting every time Peter moved his head. His windpipe had been torn apart, and bubbles popped and gurgled from the ragged hole as Peter breathed.

But it was his friend's eyes that scared Jacob most of all. They were black, and shiny, like a doll's eyes, and his pale face had the slack look of a sleeper.

Or a dead person.

Peter stared at Jacob with no sign of recognition, or any emotion, on his face.

Peter reached out and took Jacob's arm, trapped on the outside of the cellar door. To Jacob's horror, his friend bent down and began licking the blood seeping through the bandage wrapped around his arm.

Jacob yelled, and started trying to pull away, but the other boy's grip was surprisingly strong, and he held tight and continued slurping at the blood, feasting on it like a starving man. Jacob could feel himself disappearing into a wild panic. Working on instinct, he lifted his foot, and kicked at Peter's legs, raking his shoe down the other boy's shins and stamping on his feet.

Peter lifted his head and moved back, out of the way of the frenzied attack. He stepped into a patch of light, a weak square of sunshine falling across his face. The flesh on his cheek grew red, and then started blistering.

Peter grunted again, a spasm of pain distorting his slack features. He reached up and raked his fingernails across his cheek, and ribbons of ragged skin peeled off, exposing the raw meat beneath.

Forgetting about his old friend, and the warm meal of fresh blood, the Peter monster turned and began shuffling away from the strips of sunlight, still scratching at the open wound on his face.

Jacob pushed at the door again, ignoring the pain as he forced his torso and head through the gap. The sides scraped against his cheeks and then his ears. He paused for a moment, gasping with the pain and the effort, sure that he was going to rip his ears off the sides of his head if he pushed any more.

When he saw Peter begin a slow, shuffling turn back towards him, perhaps relishing the thought of slurping at Jacob's bloody wound some more, Jacob ignored the pain and began shoving his way through the gap again.

His ears feeling like they were being torn from him, Jacob's head suddenly popped through the door. He managed to get his other arm through and, gripping the door edge, dragged himself further out, until his chest was free.

The rest of his body came out more easily, and Jacob stumbled, and fell to the floor on his knees.

Peter shuffled towards him, the grunting noises growing in urgency and intensity.

Jacob stood up and shoved and pulled at the door leading outside. It was locked. He stared through the tiny squares of dirty glass, at the overgrown garden and the huge Ash tree.

Jacob turned to face the thing that used to be his friend. The twisted deformity that had once been a ten year old boy hobbled closer, blocking the passage, and the route to the front of the house. He reached out with clawed hands, desperate for Jacob's blood.

With a wild yell, swinging his arms in crazy circles, Jacob charged at the Peter monster and barrelled into him. The dead child was thrown to the side, the back of his head hitting the wall with a wet smack, and then slid to the floor.

Jacob didn't look back.

He ran into the large hallway, heavy curtains draped over the large windows creating an oppressive gloom. Jacob stood completely still, holding his breath, listening for any signs of movement. He had made so much noise pushing the cellar door open, and then fighting off the Peter monster, that he was sure he must have been heard.

The house was silent, apart from the somnolent ticking of a clock.

Jacob crept towards the front door and placed an ear against the stained glass window pane. It was cold against his skin, and he could hear the hum of traffic along the main road.

Jacob looked down, and there, protruding from the door lock, was a large, ornate handled key. The young boy gripped the key with trembling fingers, and turned it. The tumblers rotated, the sound unnaturally loud in the silence.

Not daring to believe that he might escape, Jacob twisted the door handle and pulled. The door opened a sliver, letting in a breeze of cool, fresh air.

Jacob stiffened as cold fingers caressed his cheeks, and traced a line along his jaw and down the side of his neck. The hand came to rest on his shoulder, and squeezed it.

"Oh, Jacob," a voice whispered, icy breath feathering his ear.

not scary in
a horror movie

Joe Coffin walked the length of River View Gardens with Laura. She pointed out the empty houses, and told him how the police had searched every single one, including those that were occupied by squatters. They had questioned all the residents of the estate, and widened their search net to include nearby streets, and parkland.

Anywhere that Laura could think of where the boys might have gone to play.

"What about the other boy's mother?" Coffin said.

"Brenda Marsden?" Laura said, and shook her head. Her hair was tied back in a ponytail, and stray wisps hung free, and were caught by the breeze. "That boy of hers is nothing to her, apart from a monthly cheque for child benefit. Looking after him is the only way she can afford to keep herself in cigarettes and booze."

"Did she speak to the police?"

"Yes, but she wasn't any help. She never kept tabs on Peter. He could be gone for hours on end and she would never stop to think, to worry about what might have happened to him. If I hadn't raised the alarm when Jacob didn't come home, Brenda probably still wouldn't have noticed Peter was gone."

Coffin looked up at the overcast sky. Dark clouds scudded by, heavy with the threat of more rain. Mid-afternoon, and already house lights were being switched on, and drivers were turning on their headlights. Coffin was wearing a black leather jacket over a white T-shirt, and jeans. An elderly couple crossed to the other side of the road as they approached him.

Coffin had that effect on everyone.

"I'll have a talk with some people," he said, looking at Laura. "See if anyone's heard anything. I'll talk to Craggs too, get together our own search party. They can't have just disappeared off the face of the earth, right?"

Laura placed a hand on his arm. "Thank you, Joe." Her eyes welled up with tears. "I'm sorry to have to ask you for help, so soon after . . ."

The unspoken words hung in the air between them.

"What about Tom?" Coffin said. "I saw him earlier today, he didn't mention anything about Jacob."

"Tom just thinks they've run off together, that they'll come slinking back with their tails between their legs in another couple of days."

"But Jacob's his kid. He should be worried."

Laura chewed on a fingernail, her eyes downcast. All the nails on that hand had been bitten down to the quick. Coffin remembered when Laura used to have nice fingernails. Sometimes, on an evening, he used to paint them for her, the tiny nail varnish brush looking ridiculous between his huge fingers.

"Tom isn't that bothered about Jacob," Laura said. "Jacob gives him back chat, and the two of them just argue."

"Is he hitting you again?"

"No." Laura looked up at Coffin. "I told him, if he hits me again, even just once, I'll stick a kitchen knife in his chest while he's sleeping."

"I don't know why you took him back, Laura."

"Yes, you do," she said. "I couldn't survive on my own. You know how it is, kids are expensive these days. Me and Jacob, we've got to survive somehow, and I don't want my child going to school in hand me down, faded clothes, the hems of his trousers all tattered, and the cuffs of his shirts all worn away. I needed Tom back, for the money he brings in. Nothing else."

Coffin grunted. "Tom should have brought this to Craggs the day they went missing. We probably could've found them by now."

Heavy spots of rain began falling from the dark sky.

Coffin bent down and enveloped Laura in a big, gentle hug. "Don't worry, we'll find Jacob."

Laura squeezed her eyes shut and hugged Coffin back.

"Thank you," she whispered.

* * *

Tom Mills cruised around the block a few times, keeping tabs in his rear-view mirror, before turning into No. 99's drive. His tyres crunched over the weed strewn gravel as he drove up to the house, and continued on around the side. He parked out of sight of the main road around the back. Killing the engine, he picked up the black, heavy holdall from the passenger seat. He stepped out of the car and on to the overgrown lawn, the hems of his trousers growing dark in the rain water dripping off the long grass.

Slamming the car door shut and lighting up a cigarette, Tom gazed up at the big, old house. He remembered when he was a kid, the house had already been empty for years back then. Him and his mates broke in once, daring each other to explore deeper and deeper into the house's dark corridors and shadowed rooms.

Tom had always been the hanger on, the skinny, small kid who wanted to hang with the tough boys, wanted to be cool. But none of it came naturally to him, and he was always at the back, or the brunt of the jokes and cruel jibes.

Tom had nearly pissed his pants that day in the house, but he'd gone along with it anyway. Tried to keep up a mask of bravado, cocky arrogance. But then, when he thought it might be all over, and they were going to head back outside, Joe Coffin said they should go and sit in the grand drawing room, and tell each other ghost stories.

Coffin had always been the natural leader. Even back then, when he was as skinny as a piece of string, and his dad's mates used to use him for boxing practice at his dad's gym, nobody messed with Coffin. You could see it in his eyes, not a defiance exactly, but a sense that no matter how much shit you threw at him, he'd take it.

And then he'd throw it back.

So they told ghost stories in the shrouded living room, the pale, dust sheets draped over the antique furniture adding to Tom's growing terror.

Tom had finished up squawking his eyes out, he was so scared, and the others had all laughed at him. Then they all went home, and Tom thought that come the next morning, he'd be the laughing stock of his school, for being a baby. But no one said a thing about Tom crying, and no one spoke about the house ever again.

It was like they had all been scared, each and every one of them. As though they knew that once, sometime long ago, something terrible and awful had happened there. Something so beyond the boundaries of normal human behaviour, that the echoes of it still haunted the house. And they could all feel its dreadful power, a chill deep inside their bodies, a fitful, lonely cry in the subconscious.

They were all scared, but Tom was the only one who'd cried.

Tom sucked hard on the cigarette, his pinched cheeks looking even gaunter, as he drew the nicotine deep into his lungs. That house was a nightmare all right, and here Tom was, back again. But he wasn't crying now, was he?

Tom's mobile buzzed into life, playing the theme tune to The Good, The Bad, And The Ugly.

Tom looked at the display.

"Fuck," he whispered.

He considered ignoring the call, but he knew that wouldn't do any good. If he didn't answer, they would just keep calling back. Eventually they'd get bored of being ignored, and pay him a visit.

Tom most definitely didn't want that.

"Hey," he said, his voice low.

He listened for a few moments, and then said, "Yeah, yeah, I know I did. Yeah, I know what I said, but I got it all under control . . . fuck yeah, I'll find out where it is . . . shit, keep a lid on it, will you? We're sticking with the plan, okay?"

Tom closed the connection and slipped the mobile back in his pocket, took a deep breath. He should have known better than to get involved with those people, but it had seemed like a foolproof plan at the time.

So where did it all go so fucking wrong?

Tom dropped the cigarette in the wet grass and ground his shoe over it. Rain was starting to fall from the overcast sky in fat, heavy drops. He looked up at the house again, at its blank windows and oddly shaped profile, and suddenly his childhood fears were rising within him again. For a moment he thought about turning around, getting back in the car and driving off. As far as he could get on a full tank of petrol.

"Don't be a fucking idiot," he muttered.

No matter how far he ran, it wouldn't be far enough.

Taking a firm grip on the holdall, Tom walked up to the back door and fished a key out of his pocket. He opened the door and stepped inside. His every movement became magnified in the still quietness of the house. Every time he came here, he felt like he was stepping out of his normal world, and into another existence.

One where the normal rules of life did not apply.

Tom walked slowly down the stone passageway, fighting the urge to turn and bolt back outside, climb in his car, and drive off. He pulled another cigarette out of his battered pack and placed it between his lips. He struck a match, and lit the cigarette, his hands trembling as he held the flame in place.

Perhaps they wouldn't be up yet? He was earlier than normal today, and they didn't like the daylight. He could always come back later, when it was dark. But that was bad, too. Seeing them in the night, especially Steffanie, gave him the creeps good and proper.

She'd always been a looker, Steffanie had. Tom could never work out why she married Joe Coffin, him being the ugliest bastard this side of an old man's gurning contest. But then that had been the same with Laura, too. Back when she was married to Coffin, she'd been a stunner. Then they got divorced, and she let herself go.

Especially after she had Jacob. Bloody kid was a drain on her, always pestering her for stuff, and whining about his pissy school and wanting to bring a mate round. Tom had never wanted kids, couldn't see the point of them.

But that Steffanie, yeah, she was a stunner when she was alive. But now? Tom sucked hard on his cigarette. She looked absolutely fucking amazing. But scary, too. Not scary in a horror movie, jump out of your seat and hide behind your fingers sort of way. No, there was just something unsettling about her now. Something off kilter, in a queasy, slightly arousing yet repulsive sort of way.

Tom reached the end of the passage, and pushed through the door into the entrance hall. Heavy drapes had been hung over the windows since his last visit. If they were going to black out the entire house like this, he was going to have to start bringing a torch with him.

They were usually upstairs, in the master bedroom. Once, when he had come round, they had been naked. Neither of them had been ashamed, or made any attempt to cover up. He'd told them to put some clothes on, but Steffanie, she just laughed, and walked up to him, her hips moving like a cat's. She got up real close, her lips almost on his, her breath, cold and sweet, like death, on his cheek. She traced a finger down his chest and his stomach, down to his groin, where she caressed him, until he had to step back, snapping out of a trance.

Today he could see the flickering yellow glow of candles, from the doorway to the drawing room, the door slightly ajar. He walked closer, and pushed gently at the door.

The furniture was covered in dust sheets, but fat church candles sat on the fireplace hearth, and the mantelpiece, casting an eerie orange glow over the vast room. In the flickering light, shadows moved at the outer edges of the room, giving the impression of people, or things that were not people, hiding in the corners.

But it was not the shadows that caught Tom's attention. In front of the dead fireplace, illuminated by the candlelight, Steffanie crouched over a body, slumped in a chair. Tom couldn't see the body properly, or what Steffanie was doing. He slowly approached, watching with a growing sense of horror as she placed a bowl of dark liquid on the floor beside her feet.

What was in that bowl? Was it blood?

Tom stared at Steffanie's back, unsure of what to do, how to make himself known. Saying 'Hi,' didn't seem quite appropriate in the circumstances.

He cleared his throat.

She didn't turn to him, didn't even flinch.

"Sshh," she whispered. "You'll wake him."

"Wake who?" Tom whispered.

He walked slowly, quietly, moving into a position where he could see the boy slumped in the chair.

His boy, Jacob.

His eyes were closed, and he looked pale and drawn. Steffanie was wrapping a length of soiled fabric around an ugly wound in his left forearm.

"What the fuck's going on?" Tom hissed. "Is he dead?"

Steffanie finished applying the bandage and straightened up. "No, he's not dead."

"He looks dead." Tom stared at Jacob, and ground his teeth together, his head filled with spikes of tension. "He looks . . ."

"He's alive," Steffanie replied. "For now, at least."

"That's Jacob," Tom whispered, pointing at his son, and struggling to enunciate each word. "That's my son."

"I know," Steffanie said, licking Jacob's blood from her hands. "Does this bother you? Would you like to take him home? There is still time, you can save him."

Tom couldn't seem to take his eyes off Steffanie's tongue, as it flicked in and out, from between her full, sensuous lips. Had her tongue grown longer? And her teeth, were they growing into points? Every time he saw her, she seemed to have changed a little more. She was becoming more like *him*. Even the scar across her neck was disappearing. Tom had found her and her boy lying on the blood drenched carpet in their house, their throats ripped wide open. The next time he'd seen her, when she was alive again, her throat had still been a mess, but the wound had closed up. Soon, there would be nothing left to see.

"Go on, take the boy. Don't let us stop you."

Tom turned to see Abel Mortenson standing in the living room doorway. Tom hated the sight of him. He was thickly muscular beneath his shirt, and his long, square-jawed face was handsome, yet vile at the same time. And he was smiling. Always fucking smiling, or giggling, like he knew something you didn't, and it really was very funny.

Just like the other kids at school, laughing at Tom behind his back for trying to be tough, trying to keep up with them.

Tom looked back at Jacob. He hadn't stirred, he looked so helpless, so vulnerable.

"No," Tom said, his voice struggling out of his mouth in a croak. He cleared his throat, and spoke again, louder this time. "No, do what you want with him. Fucking kid's nothing but a bloody nuisance anyway."

Abel giggled, the sound of it turning Tom's stomach, and walked over to Steffanie. He drew her close, and she draped her arms over him, and they kissed. The kiss lingered, and Abel ran his hand down Steffanie's back, and over her buttocks. She moaned softly, and rubbed herself against him, running her fingers through his black, curly hair.

Tom looked away. He felt sick in the pit of his stomach, but also slightly aroused.

"I think we're embarrassing him," Abel said, looking at Tom. "Or maybe you would like to join in? A threesome would be fun."

Tom looked back at them. Abel had pulled away. He had a spot of blood on his upper lip, and he licked it off.

Tom yelped when he felt hands tugging at his back, fingers coiling around the folds of his shirt. He yanked himself free, and whipped around to face his attacker.

"Oh, fuck me," he whispered.

Jacob's friend, Peter, gazed up at Tom with dead eyes. His face was slack, like he was asleep, and there was a nasty wound running down his cheek, like he'd scratched and scratched at it, peeling ragged strips of flesh away. His neck was open, a raw wound of glistening red meat, just like Steffanie's had been.

Peter moaned, and staggered after Tom, his arms outstretched, clawing at the air like a B-movie zombie. His chin was wet, like a dribbling baby's.

Abel giggled, and grasped Peter's shoulders, turning him around to face the opposite direction.

"Go on now," he said. "Go and play somewhere else."

The boy staggered on his way, seemingly oblivious to the direction he was headed, or that he was no longer chasing a meal of blood. Tom winced at the mass of blood matted hair on the back of his head.

"Well? Are we safe?" Abel said. "Is Coffin still looking for his family's killers, or has he found them?"

Tom swallowed. "Yeah, you're safe. Coffin whacked the two kids this morning."

Abel smiled, exposing his pointed fangs. "Good. So, no one is looking for vampires anymore?"

Tom nodded, watching as Peter staggered through the door and disappeared into the reception hall. "You're just lucky that Coffin was still in prison when you killed his wife and kid." He looked nervously at Steffanie. "If he'd been out, he'd have hunted you down, and ripped you apart. In fact, you should still lay low for a while."

"Oh, but why?" Abel said, his grotesque smile slowly fading. "You said it was sorted, that Coffin's not looking for us anymore."

"Yeah, yeah he bought it, all right. It's just, those two kids? Considering the circumstances, they were the best I could find to take the rap, but they were so fucking weedy, they looked like they couldn't fight their way out of a fucking paper bag, let alone murder anyone. Coffin's got a lot on his mind, him being fresh out of prison, and still grieving, like. But once he gets to thinking about it proper, it might not add up for him, that two skinny douchebags like them, killed his wife and kid."

"All right, then," Abel said. "We can lie low a little longer."

"You might not have to wait too long," Tom said. "There was a girl in the flat, but Coffin let her go. If she goes to the police, then Coffin's done for."

"She'll be able to identify him?"

"Unless she's fucking blind, yeah."

"And what about you, did she see you?"

Tom wiped the back of his hand across his mouth. His eyes kept flitting back to Jacob, lying in the chair, so frail, so vulnerable. "Yeah, she saw me, but that doesn't matter. Put me and Joe Coffin in the same room, you look at Coffin. Nobody notices me."

Steffanie sighed. "Oh God, I'm so bored of hiding in this house. I thought we would be free now. I want to party!"

Abel raise an eyebrow. "And here I was thinking I was keeping you quite entertained."

Steffanie giggled, and the sound of it sent another wave of nausea through Tom.

She leaned into Abel, and nuzzled her mouth into his neck, and then sucked on his ear lobe. Her hand, those long, sinuous fingers, ran down his chest and over his abdomen. She slipped her hand inside his trousers, and began caressing him.

Abel pulled her hand away. "Not now, we'll embarrass Mr Mills again. Why don't you go and feed the Father?"

Tom closed his eyes. He'd forgotten about that decrepit old creature.

"Everything all right?" Abel said. "You're looking a little pale."

Tom opened his eyes. "No, I'm fine. Absolutely fucking peachy, that's me." He dropped the holdall on the floor. "There, I brought it for you."

Abel approached Tom, but, instead of picking up the holdall, he grabbed Tom's arm, his fingers like a vice around his bicep.

"Come and say hello to the Father," he said, exposing his teeth in that repulsive smile once more. "He gets so lonely here, starved of visitors and stimulating conversation, and he so looks forward to your little visits."

Tom resisted, holding back. "No, I should be going now, before anyone notices I'm gone."

"You have a few moments, I'm sure," Abel said, and pulled him into the depths of the gloomy drawing room.

Steffanie followed them, carrying the bowl of blood.

Hidden in a shadowy corner, lost in the depths of a large, dusty wing backed armchair, sat a skeletal, wizened old man. His grey flesh was drawn tight against his skull, thin lips stretched over long, hooked teeth. A few wispy hairs clung to the skull, bony cheeks standing out against the sunken hollows beneath them. His forearms lay on the armrests, long bony fingers clutching the ends, filthy fingernails curving down, almost as long as the fingers.

He's dead, Tom thought. *He's got to be dead. Please let him be dead.*

Abel slackened his grip, and Tom yanked his arm free.

"Okay, this is lovely and all," Tom said, taking a step back and pointing at the corpse like creature in the chair. "But it looks to me like the last thing Rumple-fucking-stiltskin needs is stimulating conversation, so I'm out of here."

Before Tom could move, Abel grabbed his wrist and produced a knife. Abel slid the knife over Tom's thumb, opening up the flesh. A round, fat globule of blood swelled up on the end of his thumb.

"Hey, what the—?"

Abel held the knife to Tom's neck. "Just do as I say, Mr Mills, and then you won't get hurt. Now, on your knees."

Tom dropped to his knees in front of the seated cadaver. For an instant he felt like that little kid again, sitting with his friends in the old house, crying as he listened to the ghost story.

Abel pulled Tom's hand closer to the old man's face. Gently, he pressed his bleeding thumb against the cadaverous lips, smearing the blood over the dry flesh. The corpse's papery, sunken eyelids snapped open, and Tom flinched. The eyes were red, like the worst case ever of conjunctivitis. The corpse's lips opened enough to accept Tom's bloody thumb.

Tom closed his eyes as bile rose in his throat. But he could still hear revolting sucking noises, and feel the old man's withered tongue sliding over his thumb, and probing the wound for more blood.

"How many bags of blood in the holdall?" Abel said.

"T-twenty," Tom said, screwing his face up, trying to blot out all sounds and sensations.

"Can you get us more?"

Tom nodded, his movements jerky, like a string puppet's.

"Good." Abel let go of Tom's wrist.

He snatched his thumb out of the thing's mouth, and opened his eyes. The parchment covered skeleton in the chair stared at him, hunger keen in its red eyes, and it moaned.

Tom scrabbled away, backwards, until he bumped into a piece of furniture. He sucked in a deep breath of stagnant, damp air, willing himself not to throw up.

"What the fuck?"

Abel smiled. "He needs blood to survive."

Tom wiped sweat off his brow. "There's a fucking holdall full of bags of blood over there, why didn't you give him one of those?"

"He needs warm blood to bring him back fully to life, not the cold slop you provide for us."

"Is that right? Next time, I'll bring you a fucking microwave to heat it up with, okay?"

Tom pulled himself to his feet, not entirely sure at first if his legs would support him. He watched as Steffanie, kneeling before the skeletal creature in the chair, held the silver bowl of blood to its lips. All the way across the room, Tom could hear the thing slurping at Jacob's blood.

He looked back at Abel. "Just lay low, all right. Just stay out of fucking sight for a few days, while I think about what we do next."

Tom didn't wait for an answer. He left the room, didn't look back, couldn't bear to see Jacob again, slumped in that chair like he was already dead.

Outside, standing by his car in the wet grass, Tom started shaking. He gazed at his ghostly reflection in the rain dappled glass of the passenger door.

Fuck it! I'm like their fucking lap dog, jumping through hoops every time they tell me to. I should have asked her, I should have fucking asked her.

He looked up at a noise.

Peter was staggering aimlessly around the large garden, his feet trailing sluggishly through the long grass. And he was digging into the wound on his cheek with filthy, clawed fingers, moaning constantly.

Tom closed his eyes, trying to control his shakes.

What have I got myself into? Just what the fuck have I got myself into?

chinese whispers

After talking with Laura, Joe Coffin headed back to the flat above the Blockade. He showered, turning the water up as hot as he could bear it, and scrubbed at his body, trying to rid his flesh of prison stink.

He dried himself off with a rough, threadbare towel. Naked, he walked into the kitchen and poured himself a Jack Daniels. His head was throbbing from all the whisky he had drunk earlier in the afternoon. This was a small one, just to keep the edge off.

Coffin roamed around the flat, exploring the rooms. The living room was furnished with a settee, a sideboard with three decorative plates on stands, and an old, CRT television. He tried switching it on, but the screen stayed dead.

The kitchen was just large enough to swing a small kitten in. There was a fridge with a box freezer in the top. There was an old gas ring oven, a sink, and a single unit with cupboards above it. In relation to Coffin's size, the kitchen resembled a child's toy.

Just like the toy kitchen Steffanie had bought for Michael that one time. The boy had been eighteen months old, just a couple of months before Coffin was arrested. He'd argued with Steffanie about that toy kitchen, told her toy kitchens were for girls, not boys.

She went ballistic, told him he was a sexist, ignorant dinosaur. Told him this was the 21st century, not the 19th, and her boy wasn't going to grow up like all those other big, dumb brutes that Coffin called his friends.

A flicker of a smile passed over Coffin's face as he remembered the argument. He loved it when she stood up to him, gave as good as she got. Not like the others, all dolled up like their men wanted them to look, staying indoors cooking and cleaning and ironing and, on the rare occasions when they were allowed out of the house, not daring to look at another man for fear of a slap.

No, Steffanie was independent.

The grief gnawed keenly at him. He drained the glass of whisky, and walked into the bedroom.

A single bed took up most of the room, with a flimsy, flat pack wardrobe jammed into a corner, with just enough space to open the doors. The bed was too small for Coffin. He pulled the mattress off the base, and upended it, shoving it against the wall. He lay the mattress on the floor and threw the duvet over it.

Not ideal, but at least his feet could rest on the floor instead of hanging off the end of the bed.

He dragged a holdall off the top of the wardrobe and opened it up. After the murder, once the police had finished at the house, somebody went and collected his clothes so he didn't have to go back there.

Coffin hadn't ever wanted to go back inside that house.

But he knew he had to, at some point. There were memories there, of his life with Steffanie, and Michael. Mementos, photographs, Michael's childish scrawls and finger paintings. His clothes, his toys, and teddy bears. That blanket he carried everywhere with him, blue with a spotty cartoon dog on it, and its feathered edges which Michael loved brushing against his face.

Coffin took a deep breath. Held it. Let it go.

He'd go back at some point, but maybe not just yet.

Perhaps tomorrow he'd ask one of the guys to go over to the house and get his bike, his Harley Davidson Fat Boy. All those months in prison, unable to get out, on the road. Felt like he'd been going insane some days, about ready to murder someone, anyone.

But he'd held it together, and now more than ever, he needed to climb on that bike, and ride.

Maybe ride out as far as he could, and not come back.

He got dressed. White T-shirt and jeans, what he always wore. The weather was turning colder now, so when he went outside he might wear his scuffed leather jacket.

Fashion had never been his thing. Not even after he met Steffanie.

When he was ready, he pounded down the stairs and strode through the pub. He drew glances from people sat at tables and the bar. One or two voices shouted, "Hey, Joe! Good to see you back," and one voice said, "Sorry about your family, Joe."

He nodded an acknowledgement and headed outside. The street lights were surrounded by a misty halo, and the air felt damp against Coffin's face. The shops had closed up, some of them dark, some of them with their window displays illuminated. Young couples, hand in hand, or arms around each other, sauntered along the pavements, giggling and chatting, dressed up for a night out. A gang of male youths approached, all gelled, spiky hair and attitude, shouting insults and laughing. When they saw Coffin they went quiet, and crossed the road.

Joe Coffin strode down the high street, and turned right onto Hagley Road, headed for the city centre.

* * *

After Terry Wu got taken care of, and Craggs bought the nightclub, he had the name changed to Angels. One of the guys had tried explaining to him that Angellicit was a play on words. Angel, denoting beauty and purity, and Illicit, meaning forbidden or naughty.

Craggs didn't like it when people tried explaining stuff to him. He told Coffin, "The way I see it, I don't understand first time, I ain't interested. This piece of shit, he tried explaining it to me. I told him I wasn't interested, but still he kept on at me, gave me a fuckin headache so bad I wanted to pull a gun and shoot him in the face."

The 'piece of shit' wound up cleaning toilets for a month.

Craggs had been unhappy with the takings at Angellicit for a long time. Terry Wu was nothing but a 'fat, lazy, chink bastard' according to Craggs, and if he was in charge of the club, they would be doing three or four times the business.

Craggs decided he wanted in. He would buy the club, change the name, and move himself into the suite of rooms above the nightclub. All he needed to do was get rid of Terry Wu.

The double doors had neon wings across them, lit up in blue and gold. Two big black guys stood on the steps, flexing their muscles at each other through their tight, black tees, the angel wings illustrated in white across their chests.

They stood back enough to let Coffin through, and one of them clapped him on the back as he walked past.

"Yo, Joe, sorry to hear bout the family, man."

"Yeah, thanks, Clevon," Coffin said, pausing long enough to grip his hand in a show of solidarity.

"Anything you need, man, anything at all, you just let me know, I'll be there," Clevon said.

Coffin patted him on the shoulder and walked through the entrance. Clevon was the youngest, and newest member of the Slaughterhouse Mob, and Coffin had taken an instant liking to him. He also knew he was too good hearted for a life in the Mob. Coffin had intended to sit down and have a chat with Clevon one day, maybe try and persuade him to find another vocation in life.

Coffin walked past the cloak room and toilets, and through the double doors into the club. It was early, and most of the tables were empty. Some crappy, European electronic disco music pounded through the club's mostly empty space, and a large breasted girl, wearing only a thong and a forced smile, gyrated around a pole. A middle aged man in a business suit watched her through hooded eyes, listlessly twirling a beermat around and around with his thick fingers.

Coffin made his way to the back of the club, and the dancing girl waved at him as he passed the stage. Coffin gave her a weary wave back, and pushed through a door marked, 'Private'. His way was immediately blocked by another of Craggs' bouncers, wearing the regulation Angels tee, all steroid enhanced muscles and tatts. Coffin could spot the steroid abusers every time, with their elongated jaws and high-pitched voices.

"Oh, hey, Joe, didn't realise it was you," the bouncer said.

He stepped back, eyes on the floor, like he didn't know what to say next.

Coffin pushed past him and took the stairs two at a time.

Mortimer Craggs was in his office, sat behind his mahogany desk, in his oversized leather swivel chair, just like Coffin knew he would be. He had on a velvet dressing gown, and he was smoking a huge cigar. The old man looked like he had shrunk since Coffin last saw him, like he'd aged ten years in the last six months.

But when he saw Coffin, his eyes lit up, and he jumped to his feet and strode around his desk. He grabbed Coffin in a hug, slapping him on the back, and saying, "It's good to see you, son, real good to see you."

Coffin enveloped the old man in a hug.

Craggs stood back and slapped Coffin on the chest, and spoke to a blond woman sitting cross legged in a chair, painting her toenails.

"Hey, Velvina, this boy here, he's salt of the earth, he is. Bout the only fucker I can trust these days, that's for sure. Hey, you listening to me?"

Velvina looked up from her toenails, her mouth moving like she was a cow chewing the cud. Her eyes were glassy and unfocused.

"Ah, forget about her," Craggs said, waving his hand in dismissal, and turning his back on her. He put his arm around Coffin's shoulders. He had to stretch, and it looked uncomfortable, but he did it, and he guided Coffin to a chair. "Let me get you a drink, what are you having?"

"Whisky," Coffin said.

"Of course, whisky," Craggs said. "That's what you like, Joe, ain't it? Listen, I've got something special for you, you've never had this before."

The old man walked over to a huge globe atlas, like something out of an old movie about Victorian adventurers, and opened it up. Inside were several bottles and glasses. Craggs took one of the bottles and two whisky glasses, and poured them both a drink.

"I've been saving this, Joe, for you." Craggs handed Coffin a whisky glass, the amber liquid glowing in the soft light. "It's a Glenfarclas, aged fifty years, would you believe it?"

Coffin sipped the whisky. It had a sweet sherry aftertaste, and spread warmth from his gullet and through his chest.

"Poor bastards who barrelled this are probably dead now. Imagine that, Joe, being a part of making something so special, something that has to be left alone for time to do its work, for so long, that you know you won't be alive to see the fruits of your labour. I wonder what that feels like."

Craggs lifted the glass to his nose and breathed in the whisky aroma. Then he took a deep swallow, and closed his eyes.

Coffin swigged his whisky back and placed the heavy, cut glass on the desk.

Craggs opened his eyes, and Coffin realised he'd been wrong. Craggs hadn't shrunk, he was still the man Coffin remembered. He'd lost some weight, maybe, and he was a little more stooped. But, looking into his eyes, Coffin could still see the man Craggs had always been. The killer, the head of the Slaughterhouse Mob, the most powerful criminal gang boss in the city.

"Tom told me he found the scumbags who killed poor Steffanie and Michael," Craggs said. "Have you taken care of that, Joe?"

"Yeah, I took care of them this morning," Coffin said.

Craggs nodded, appreciatively. "Good, I'm glad to hear it, Joe. Tom wanted to do it himself, while you were still locked up. I said no. I said, wait till Joe gets out, let him take care of it."

Coffin looked over at the girl painting her toenails. "You, get out."

The girl looked up at him and pouted. "Aw, do I have to?"

Without turning to look at her, his voice low, Craggs said, "Joe Coffin asked you to leave. Don't make me have to ask, too."

Pouting some more, the girl took her time replacing the brush in the nail varnish bottle. When she stood up, Coffin caught a glimpse of silk red panties beneath the over-sized T-shirt. She padded barefoot across the office, and left, closing the door softly behind her.

Craggs patted Coffin on the arm. "What's wrong, Joe? You look tense, like you got something on your mind. Why don't you come and sit down, we'll talk about it."

The two men sat down on leather sofas, facing each other.

Coffin leaned forward, putting his elbows on his knees. "Those two kids, I killed them. The one, I blew his brains out. The other, I filled his chest with bullets, kept shooting until the gun was empty and he looked like a piece of bloody meat."

Craggs nodded. "That's good, Joe. That's how it should be. They murdered your family, they had it coming."

"No, I don't think they did," Coffin said.

The words hung in the silence between them, for a long second.

"What do you mean, Joe?" Craggs said.

"I'm not sure those two kids had anything to do with the attack on my wife and son."

Craggs stared at Coffin through eyes narrowed down to slits. "Why do you say that?"

"Tom said to me, he said, those two were members of a vampire cult, liked to pretend they were vampires, filed their teeth down to points, maybe even drank each other's blood sometimes. He said, they were wasted on drugs when they broke into our house, that they lost all control, and savaged my family."

Craggs nodded slowly, leaning forward and tapping ash off his cigar into an ashtray. "That's right, that's what Tom told me."

"Mort, those two kids? Steffanie would have dealt with them like two naughty schoolboys. The way I heard, Steffanie and Michael, they looked like they'd been attacked by a pack of wild animals."

Craggs puffed on his cigar for a few moments, head tilted back while he thought about what Coffin had said.

"People exaggerate, you know?" he said, finally. "Tom told someone what he saw, he tells the next guy, with a few embellishments, and so on. What do you call it, there's a term for it, right?"

"Chinese whispers."

"Yeah, that's it. Chinese whispers. By the time you got told the story, it probably looked nothing like the story Tom told that first guy, you know what I'm saying?"

"Yeah, I know what you're saying," Coffin said.

"This kind of thing, Joe, losing your family, it'll eat away at you, like a fucking cancer, you let it. You took out their killers, you got your revenge and they got what was coming to them. I know it's early days Joe, Steffanie and Michael in freshly turned ground, but you got to start thinking about moving on at some point."

Coffin cracked his knuckles, looked at the floor, the dark wood varnished and polished so much, he could almost see his face in it. "If there's a chance I got it wrong, I took out those two kids for no reason, I've got to find out, Mort. I need to know, because if Steffanie and Michael's killers are still out there, I need to spill more blood."

The old man stood up and walked around the coffee table, stood by Coffin, and placed a gentle hand on his shoulder. "I know that, Joe, I do. I'll have another talk with Tom, find out where he got his information from. But right now, you need to go home, Joe, get some sleep. This has been a big day for you, first day out of prison, and all."

Coffin looked up at the old man. How old was he now? Eighty? Eighty-one? Craggs had always been so powerful, so full of life and vitality. So strong. And that strength still lived inside him, Coffin could see that now. Despite the growing frailty of his ageing body, the fire still burned in his eyes.

"One more thing, Mort. Laura came to see me today, said her boy's gone missing."

Craggs nodded. "I know. I've had the guys out looking for him. Kid's disappeared off the face of the fucking earth."

"Laura doesn't know you've got people looking for him. She thinks she's on her own here."

"I thought Tom would have told her. Those two are still together, right?"

"Yeah, they're still together. Tom doesn't care for them, though. Doesn't care for either of them. I doubt he cares one way or the other about Jacob, and if he comes back."

Craggs sucked on his cigar, the end glowing bright orange, the crackle of burning tobacco loud in the silence of the vast office. "Don't be too hard on Tom. He looked after Steffanie and Michael while you were inside. He's a good man."

Coffin shook his head. "How can you say that, after what he did to Laura?"

"He's got a temper on him, especially when he's drunk. But we had a chat about that, Joe, you remember. Hell, you were there. The drink takes him, and turns him into something mean and nasty. That never happened to you, Joe?"

Coffin twisted his hands together, trying to ease the tension out of them. Trying to forget how he had used those hands sometimes. "I've done some bad things, stuff I regret when I've woken up in the morning, and I've been sober enough to remember. But Laura?"

"Let Tom be, Joe. He knows what he's done. He won't do it again."

Coffin stood up. "I'm going to take your advice, old man. Go back to the flat, get some shut eye."

Craggs punched him on the arm and grinned. "Less of the old man. It came right down to it, I could still drink you under the table."

Coffin smiled. "Yeah, I bet you could."

Coffin headed back outside. The misty, night air had turned into a drizzle. Coffin pulled the collar of his jacket up around his neck, and picked up his pace as he walked back to the Blockade.

The sound of his footsteps echoed through the empty streets. All the drinkers and clubbers had gone inside, and there were no cars on the road, and for a few moments he felt like he was the last man on earth, and he was destined to roam the empty streets alone, with nothing but painful memories to keep him company.

And that seemed a fitting penance.

emma on display

Despite the cold evening air, Tom Mills was burning hot. Parked outside his house, the engine off, he gripped the steering wheel, his teeth clenched, sweat running down his face.

How could he go inside and face Laura, after what he had seen? Stupid, fucking kid, why did he have to go and get himself involved? Tom closed his eyes, tired of looking at the rain spattered windscreen, the streetlights refracted through the raindrops. He snapped them open again. In the darkness behind his eyelids all he could see was Jacob's frail, tiny body, draped over that chair whilst Steffanie bandaged up his arm.

He had looked dead. Steffanie said he wasn't, but the poor little bastard couldn't be far off. And what about the other kid, what was his name? Jeremy? Peter? Yeah, that was it, Peter Marsden.

What had happened to him? Was he dead?

What had Abel and Steffanie been thinking? Fucking coppers were crawling all over the city looking for those two kids. Might as well put a fucking sign up over the house, in red, flashing neon, 'HERE WE ARE, COME AND GET US. WE KIDNAP CHILDREN AND DRINK THEIR BLOOD'.

Tom wiped sweat off his forehead, his hand trembling slightly.

But then Abel didn't strike Tom as being the sharpest tool in the box. Maybe that was typical of his kind. All fired up in the sex department, but not much going on upstairs.

The first time he'd met Abel, Tom had been falling down drunk, at the end of a long, long night. Craggs had warned him off the drink after that incident with Laura, backed up by his pet dog, Coffin, but sometimes Tom couldn't resist. With a shitty life like his, who could blame him for the occasional binge? So he'd been out, drinking himself into a state of oblivion. Staggering back home at some unearthly hour in the morning, he'd needed a piss. He'd ducked down an alley, and done his business, and it was only when he was zippering himself back up that he noticed the noises.

Sucking, slurping noises, like his old dad used to make, at the end of his life when the cancer had ravaged his body and taken all his teeth. All he could do was eat soup, and suck on orange slices. The slurping and dribbling used to make Tom feel sick, but his mother never let up, said it was his duty to look after his dad after all he'd done for him. Fucking fifteen years old, he should've been out with his mates, not spoon feeding a toothless cripple, and wiping up his dribble and snot.

Tom had walked further into the dark alley, using the wall as support. Didn't give a thought as to what he might find, he was curious, that was all. Drunk, and curious.

The alley was so dark, Tom almost tripped over the shadowed shape, huddled on the floor. It was a man, his back to Tom, holding something to his face, and sucking at it. The man hadn't noticed he had company.

Tom pulled out his matches, and struck a light. As he held up the lit match, the man turned, startled by the sudden noise. In the weak, flickering light, Tom saw the man's mouth, turned down in a grimace, smeared with dark blood. In his hands he held the butchered remains of a cat.

Tom's first instinct was to run, but the beer had taken its toll, and his legs refused the impulse to flee back down the alley, and into the city centre, where he might find normal people, not cat eating crazies.

The man dropped the cat and stood up, and when he rose to his full height, Tom could see he was powerful and lithe, a little like a cat himself. A part of Tom awakened at that moment, a door opened in the depths of his subconscious, into a room that Tom had never known existed before. And he found himself strangely attracted to this man, and yet repulsed at the same time.

Now he feared he was in too deep, had involved himself in something he should have left alone. After what he had seen this afternoon, back at the house, Tom wished he had never set foot in that alley, never gone investigating those sounds. He should have just gone home, slept off the booze. Then, the following morning he'd have woken up with a killer hangover, and got on with his miserable shitty life, not realising how close he'd come to fucking it all up so completely.

But no. He had to go and play at being Lieutenant fucking Columbo, didn't he?

Tom wiped his sleeve across his forehead. The car windows were all steamed up. Fucking hell, why was he so hot? Perhaps he had a fever, maybe he was coming down with something. Wouldn't that be fucking great, coming down with flu, or some other shit, right now when he needed to be sharp.

Tom licked his lips. What he needed was a drink or two. Something to calm his nerves, try and take the edge off the image of his boy, so pale and weak, and that awful wound in his arm. He'd never had any time for the little weed, and he knew the kid hated him back.

So why the hell was Tom so bothered what happened to Jacob?

Why did he even give a shit?

* * *

Emma Wylde turned the car onto her drive, and parked in front of the house. The study light was on, the desk lamp illuminating Nick Archer at his desk, intently studying an open file. The rest of the house was in darkness, which meant that he had done nothing but work in the study since coming home.

Emma bipped the car locked, and pulled her bag over her shoulder. With a story to write up about the two missing boys, to go with the interview she hoped to get tomorrow with Laura Mills, it didn't look like Emma would be seeing much of her husband tonight.

Just the same as any other night, then.

"Hello?" she called, as she dumped her bag in the hall, and hung her coat on the wooden coat stand Nick had bought from an antique shop in Ludlow last year. He loved collecting old things, and she sometimes teased him that he was an antique, too.

"Hi, Ems!" Nick called back. "There's a fresh pot of coffee on the go in the kitchen."

"Thanks." Emma entered the kitchen and switched on the lights. Chrome units reflected the light, whilst the walnut panelled doors softened the room, making a nice contrast with the ultra-modern style of the kitchen.

Emma and Nick lived in a Victorian, double fronted detached. The house had fallen into ruin over the years, and was in a sorry state when they bought it. Emma had fallen in love with it on their first viewing. With her imagination and eye for style, and Nick's salary as a DCI supplying the money, they transformed it into a modern, smart home, whilst still keeping many of the original features.

Nick had left two mugs by the coffee maker, and a chocolate truffle, wrapped in gift paper and tied with a little bow. Emma smiled. This was a tradition of his, whenever he was home first. It had started not long after they moved in together, after a holiday in Paris. Each lunchtime, they had visited a tiny café on Boulevard St Germaine, where they had drunk coffee and eaten chocolate truffles.

Emma unwrapped the chocolate and popped it into her mouth. She chewed thoughtfully, enjoying the sensation and taste of the chocolate melting over her tongue. How many chocolate truffles did that make this week? Was this her third? Emma sighed. If she was going to keep her weight down she would have to start getting home earlier.

She poured the coffee and took the steaming mugs into the study.

"Hey." Emma placed the mugs on the study desk, bent down and kissed Nick on the lips.

"Hey, yourself," Nick said, and licked his lips. "Hmm, chocolate."

"As always, thank you." Emma smiled. "I swear you're trying to fatten me up."

Nick took his reading glasses off, and placed them on the open file. "Not a chance, not with all that running you do."

Emma swivelled Nick's chair around so that his back was to the desk, and sat on his lap.

"How was your day?" she said, running her fingers gently down his cheek. "Catch any bad guys today?"

"Not today, but it was fine." Nick wrapped his arms around her. "How about yours? Any major breaking news stories that I need to know about?"

"As if I'd tell you," she said, nuzzling her mouth up against his ear. "What about you? Any new leads on cases that I can go public with?"

"You already know the answer to that one, Ems." Nick ran his hands up inside Emma's shirt, his fingers finding the hook on her bra strap.

"Yeah, yeah, I'll be the first to know about it at the press conference."

Her lips found his, and they kissed, long and lingering.

"What do you think you're doing back there, anyway?" she whispered, her lips brushing his as she spoke.

"You're the investigative reporter, can't you figure it out by yourself?"

"Very funny," Emma said. "You seem to be struggling a bit. Need any help?"

The bra strap popped open.

"Nope, I think I got it."

"You do realise we're on public display here, don't you?" Emma said, glancing at the window.

"Maybe we should go upstairs to the bedroom."

Emma kissed him again, heat rising from her stomach and into her chest as his hands went exploring under her shirt.

"Seriously, though," she said, growing breathless now, "have you got any leads on those two missing kids?"

Nick pulled back. "I don't believe you."

"What?"

"Do you always have to be on the job, Emma?"

"Hey, I just asked you a question, that's all. One simple, fucking question."

"Aw, come on, Ems, you know how much I hate it when you swear."

Emma stood up, reached under her shirt and clipped her bra back on. "Not you as well. I've already had this shit from Mr Modern, Karl, today. What is it with you men, are you living on a different planet from me? Us girls, we're even allowed to vote now, did you know that?"

Nick threw his hands in the air. "All right, all right! Pardon me for being a sexist pig!"

He swivelled around to face his desk, put his glasses back on, and hunched over the open file, illuminated by the glow of the angle poise lamp. Emma stood behind him, cursing herself for losing her temper so easily. She placed her hands on his shoulders, and started massaging the muscle, all bunched up and tense.

"Hey, I'm sorry," she said.

"Sure," Nick said, not looking around.

Emma leaned forward slightly to look at the file he was reading. She saw the name Joe Coffin. She bit her lip, wanting to ask what Nick was working on, but knowing that it would only make things worse between them.

But still, Joe Coffin. Hadn't he got out of jail today?

Shit. Just don't do it, don't ask him.

She needed to take drastic action, get her mind off her job. Taking a deep breath, she stepped back, and pulled her shirt off, and then her bra, dropping them on the floor. She pulled her trousers down, and her panties, and stepped out of them. She grabbed hold of Nick's chair and swivelled him around to face her, and sat on his lap, straddling his thighs.

The look of anger at being disturbed, swiftly disappeared from Nick's face, replaced by a smile. Emma took his glasses off, and put them on the desk. She started unbuttoning his shirt, whilst kissing him.

"We're still on public display," Nick said breathlessly, between kisses.

Emma tugged at his belt.

"Yeah? So what?" she said.

someone is digging

When she opens her eyes, the darkness is all consuming. She is lying down, confined in a small space. She knows she is trapped, although she does not know why, or where. Yet she feels no fear.

This lack of fear is interesting. Once, in a previous life perhaps, she feels that she would have been terrified, trapped in this narrow, enclosed space. But not now. For the moment, she is content to lie here, exploring the exciting new sensations that are awakening inside of her.

First, there is her vision. She knows that, no matter how long she lies here, for an eternity even, her eyes will never adapt, that she is blind in this place.

And yet she can see.

This is not a normal way of seeing, not one that she has experienced before. She can see, or rather sense, the soil, and the grass, the monuments to the dead, and the stars in the sky. The moist, earthy smell of the soil is strong, and she can hear the tiny creatures wriggling and burying their way towards her.

All of her senses are heightened. She is more alive to the world around her than she has ever been, as though she has wandered through life with her eyes closed, and hands over her ears. She can feel the weight of the sky above her. She can sense the stars, and the universe stretching out to infinity, but she is no longer insignificant beneath its enormity.

Her breath catches in the back of her throat, a little cry, like a lover responding to her partner's touch. She feels the pulse of a new life force, surging through her from the pit of her stomach, and outwards in hot waves of pleasure. She begins to writhe and squirm in the confined space, an electric tingle coursing through her nerves. She clenches her fists, her long fingernails digging into the soft flesh of her palms, and yet she feels no pain. Arching her back, she opens her mouth, panting, needing the exquisite pulsations to stop, and yet hungry for more.

She reaches a moment of total abandonment, her every muscle taut with desire and pain, corruption and hunger, and she is nothing, and she is everything, and then the waves of power begin to dissipate, her muscles relax, and she is left drained and weak.

And with a taste for blood.

Her tongue begins exploring her mouth, running over her teeth and her lips, like she has never explored her mouth before. The nerve endings on her tongue are now so sensitive, the sensation is almost painful. Her teeth feel sharp, like a predator's teeth, and her lips are sensual and full.

She needs blood. She craves to fill her mouth with warm blood, its coppery taste shooting sharp pangs of desire through her stomach, and she can imagine the sensation of it sliding down her throat, dribbling from between her lips as the red liquid pulses into her mouth, too much to swallow and yet she can't stop sucking at it, needing more, yet more.

She lifts a hand to her throat, dizzy with desire, and her fingers find the wound. She begins exploring the jagged rip in her throat, the torn edges of her flesh sewn roughly together. She wants to rip the stitches out, and insert her fingers inside.

And she remembers.

The man, tapping on her window.

She had a name then, but the name is of no consequence now. She forgot her name the moment she saw him, when she looked into his eyes. His flesh was pale, like the moon, but his eyes were dark, filled with knowledge and pleasure and wickedness.

Let me in, he said. *Let me in.*

And she did let him in, and he entered her, and despoiled her, and in that moment of ecstasy and terror, she knew that she had lost everything, including herself, that she had stepped through a doorway into another world, of cold pleasure and depraved abandonment, and she could never come back.

And the darkness swallowed her.

There is movement above her. A footfall, a disturbance in the packed earth.

She places the palm of her hand against the roof of her prison, only inches from her face. The surface is soft, like velvet, but there is cold resistance behind it.

A thought occurs to her.

Is she in a coffin?

Tremors shiver through her hand and down her arm.

Someone is digging.

* * *

Steffanie's eyes opened. She could feel the pull of the night, the moon behind the clouds, the eternity of stars behind that blanket of grey she used to call a sky. The need to slip outside, to prowl through the city's streets, or leap across the roof tops, to *hunt*, was strong upon her.

But Abel had forbidden her. He understood the need, it bedevilled him, too, making his flesh crawl with desire until he scratched and scratched, and then pounced upon her. She fed him, however she could. Her blood was still pure enough that he could drink from her, but not for long. Another few days, and her body fluids would be poisonous.

And then she would be just like him.

Abel said they needed to stay hidden. For a while longer, at least.

But she didn't know how much longer she could stand it, cooped up in this house, forbidden to explore the night.

Steffanie sat up, pushing her long, red hair from her face. She ran her fingers over her lips, so fat and full, and her teeth, so sharp now.

She had been dreaming again. Always the same dream, that moment in her coffin, in the ground, when she was reborn.

Abel had come to her, his instinct telling him she was ready. He had dug through the moist, freshly turned earth, and pulled her from her tomb, birthed her into the night, blinking and staring in wonder like a newborn.

Abel cradled her in his arms, sitting on the damp ground, amongst the tombstones. She reached for the stars, her arms white as alabaster, her fingers like claws against the night sky, beneath the light of the full moon and a million stars. Abel pulled her funeral clothes from her, and lay her naked on a tomb. And, naked too, he climbed on top of her. She bit and scratched him as he thrust at her like an animal, the moon illuminating their pale, writhing bodies.

She had not known that she was once Steffanie. Neither had she remembered she once had a husband, and a son. It was a mystery to her when Abel took her to the grave next to hers, and looked almost sadly up on it.

He was too young to turn. The night could not claim him, but at least he shall have peace.

She remembered nothing of her old life.

But the last few days the memories had been rushing back. Images and sounds, snatches of conversations, all piling on top of one another in fragments. She remembered she once had a son, and a husband, Joe Coffin.

She remembered a wedding, with only her and Coffin and the registrar in attendance. And she remembered giving birth to her son, the pain and the blood, and the fear, that everything was changing, that nothing would ever be the same.

Other snatches of memory. Dancing, with people watching her. A woman, asking her questions. A fight in a pub, Joe Coffin pummelling someone until his face was a bloody pulp.

And something else.

Something hidden.

Something important.

Why were the memories flooding back? Why now?

It was that boy, Jacob.

Having him here had triggered something. The rush of memories began as a trickle, when the boy first whispered her name.

Steffanie.

As though he could evoke pity in her heart by speaking that name she once used, in her old life.

Steffanie.

As though she could save him.

He knew, when he looked into her eyes, the boy knew she was no longer Steffanie.

Steffanie was dead.

* * *

Tom cursed loudly as someone jostled his elbow, and the top of his Saxon Gold spilled over the edge of his glass, and dribbled down the side.

He looked around, intending to give whoever had bumped him a mouthful, but there were too many people, all struggling for the bar, before last orders. Tom sat down heavily at a table, squashed between an enormous young woman with pink hair, and a tattoo of a barcode on her left shoulder, and an old man with liver spotted hands talking to his friend.

Tom looked at the barcode, wondering why someone would do that. Was it a personal statement of some kind? Did she consider herself little more than a number, encoded for digital devices? Was she commenting on the future, or maybe making some sort of political statement?

Tom considered taking out his smartphone and scanning the barcode.

Perhaps she was a prostitute, and her website would open up on his phone, with a list of her services and prices.

Or perhaps she would turn around and see what he was doing, and give him a mouthful.

Tom should have known better than to come to The Headless Lady on a Friday night. All he'd wanted was a quiet drink, some time to himself, to get as drunk as possible, as quickly as possible. But the pub was noisy, and had begun to hurt his head, and it was hot.

Tom looked at his pint of beer, his seventh of the evening. He had a good buzz on, but still the image of his son, so deathly pale, remained fixed in his mind. Tom wanted to obliterate any memory of him and his life. How could he look at Laura, knowing what he had seen?

How could he look at himself?

Tom took a long swallow of the cold beer. Jacob was nothing to him, he just had to keep telling that to himself. The kid had been nothing but a pain in the arse from the moment he was born. Crying and whingeing, always needing Laura's attention. As soon as that scrawny kid was in her arms, still covered in crap, it was like Tom didn't exist anymore.

From that point on, everything was about the kid. He needed a feed, he needed his nappy changing, he needed burping, he needed bathing, he needed a cuddle.

What about me? Tom had thought. *When do I get a fucking cuddle? Preferably in bed, with no clothes on.*

Fuck. Laura wouldn't let him anywhere near her the first few months after the birth. Said she was tired, said she had a pounding headache, said she didn't feel like it. And when he did see her naked, she still had her baby belly, looked like she was pregnant again, and she repulsed him, turned him off like he'd been dropped in a bath of ice cold water.

It was all the kid's fault. Laura should've got an abortion, like he told her to. He never wanted kids, they were never supposed to have children, that's what they agreed when they got married.

No kids.

Just the two of us.

Fuck.

Tom took another swallow of his beer.

He'd thought it would get better as the boy grew up, but it just seemed to get worse. The kid grew more demanding, wanting toys, wanting to be played with, Laura even saying one time that maybe Tom should read the kid a fucking bedtime story once in a while.

Not a chance.

And then there was that time a few years back, when he came home steaming drunk, and she was waiting for him in bed, and it was dark, so he couldn't see her saggy belly with its stretch marks, and for once he'd managed to get it up, but then it was over too quickly, and had it even been worth it?

But she'd tricked him. She wanted another kid, all along she'd wanted a sister or brother for the kid, and when he found out that she was pregnant again, he'd been so furious he could hardly even think. He'd bottled that fury up for weeks, until that afternoon he came home, pissed off his head, and all the anger exploded inside of him, and he had to let it out.

The last thing Tom remembered was him and Laura arguing in the kitchen, screaming at each other, his head pounding like an artery was about to pop.

The next thing he knew, Laura was lying on the floor in a puddle of blood, and Tom was standing over her, panting like he'd been in a fight, and someone was pounding on the door, and the kid was standing by him, punching and slapping him on the back, and crying.

And Tom knew it was bad.

He lifted his glass and drained the rest of it. Time to go home. Laura would be in bed by now, and he wouldn't have to face her. And in the morning, if he got out of the house quick, like he had something urgent to attend to, he wouldn't have to listen to her crying about Jacob, and how Tom could be doing more to help find him.

Because, God help him, he couldn't stand it if she did that. The way he felt now, if she asked him about Jacob, he'd just spill his guts and tell her everything.

Tom stood up and pushed his way through the crowded pub. Outside, a sudden rush of dizziness and weakness overcame him, and he had to lean against a wall, afraid that he might fall over.

Tom rested his head against the wall and closed his eyes. His head was pounding and his heart hammering in his chest.

All I need now is a fucking heart attack, wouldn't that finish the day off like a fucking dream?

Slowly the pounding in his head subsided, and his heartbeat slowed down. When he had calmed down enough that he could think clearly, he opened his eyes. It was late, and traffic was light on the roads. That was good. Tom had intended walking home, he wasn't fit to sit behind the wheel of a car, but now that he was outside, thinking about that long walk home, he decided to drive.

Tom rubbed wearily at his face. Shit, all he wanted to do was climb into bed and forget about everything. What a mess.

Tom walked slowly to his car, and spent some time concentrating on fitting the key into the ignition. He turned on the engine, and switched on the headlights, and then lay his forehead against the steering wheel and closed his eyes.

After taking a few deep breaths, willing himself to stay awake, he sat up, put the car into first gear, released the handbrake, and drove slowly out of the car park. He took the curve too wide as he turned right onto Hagley Road, and the passenger side wheels mounted the pavement. Cursing, he overcorrected, and jumped as a car horn blared behind him, and the driver flashed his headlights.

The other car accelerated past, the driver flicking the V at Tom.

When he finally parked up, Tom realised he had driven the rest of the journey on autopilot. He had no memory of the drive, and for all he knew he could have left a trail of crashed cars and injured pedestrians in his wake.

But the night was quiet, there was no sound of police cars in pursuit, or angry drivers chasing him on foot, their mangled cars left stranded in the middle of the road.

Tom climbed slowly out of the car. He pushed the door shut, and locked it with his key fob, the red lights flashing twice, on and off.

He looked up, and his eyes widened in dismay.

"Fuck," he whispered, white clouds of breath streaming from his mouth.

Driving on autopilot, his mind lost in an alcoholic fog, Tom's unconscious had taken him to the wrong place.

He walked unsteadily through the gate and along the path. In the dark, his sodden mind struggling to make connections, he stumbled along uneven ground, and tripped over stones hidden by the night, until he eventually found what he was looking for.

Steffanie's grave, a wreath placed over it. Tom had filled that grave back in, after Abel had dug Steffanie free. It had taken him over a couple of hours, but his hands had been trembling, and he hardly had the strength to shovel the dirt back into the hole.

Seeing Steffanie alive had knocked him for six. Tom had never really been able to fully believe that Abel was a vampire, despite what he had seen. But looking at Steffanie, looking as beautiful as ever, and yet queasily different, too, standing before him, risen from the dead, had shaken Tom to the core.

He had returned, and filled in Steffanie's desecrated grave, hiding the evidence that it had been tampered with.

And he'd done a good job. Looking at it now, no one would know that she wasn't there anymore.

But Michael's grave.

That was different.

Tom approached it slowly, hardly able to believe his eyes. He knelt down beside the hole in the grave, soil scattered around it, like whoever had been digging had been working furiously, in a panic, or a rage.

Tom placed his hands on the ground, beside the hole, and leaned forward, peering into it. The coffin lid had been ripped open, splinters of wood lying in the empty casket.

Little Michael's body was not there.

Tom lay on his back beside the grave and closed his eyes.

Had someone come and stolen Michael's body?

Or had the little boy come back to life, and dug himself free?

peter goes home

Brenda Marsden sat up, her heart hammering, blood pulsing through her head. The heavy duvet slipped off the bed, and Brenda shivered. The cold prickled at her flesh. Had she screamed, when she sat up, so violently wrenched from her sleep? She took a deep breath, trying to calm her heart, still thumping away in her ribcage. Was she having a heart attack?

With a trembling hand, she reached out to her bedside cabinet. Fingers fumbled with her lamp's cable, until she found the switch, and flicked on the light.

She squinted in the sudden glare, placing a hand over her eyes. The bed sheet felt clammy and cold. Had she wet herself? Was that why she had woken up so suddenly? Had it been her mind's futile attempt at stopping her body from betraying her, from embarrassing her?

Brenda ran the flat of her palm over the damp sheet. No, she hadn't pissed in the bed, after all. She'd been sweating, as she thrashed about beneath the heavy, winter duvet. She remembered feeling hot and feverish, kicking out, pushing and pulling at the cover, as though trying to fight her way out of a nightmare.

Already the details of the dream had fled, leaving her only with a sense of having been utterly terrified. The terror still lingered, in her chest, in her stomach, the ends of her fingers tingling, and the inside of her mouth thick and sticky.

She pulled the duvet off the bedroom floor and over herself, wrapping it around her body like a protective cocoon.

Only a dream. I just need to calm down, forget about it.

Brenda peered at her clock. Her eyesight was getting worse. Every day now it seemed like her visible world was shrinking, imprisoning her in an indistinct blur of light and shadow. She should go to the optician, but what would they do? Just try and sell her some glasses, that's all. Like everybody else in life, they just wanted her money. The bloody government, the council, all those bloody salesmen on the doorstep, and the Jehovah's Witnesses, even the men she sometimes had up here in her bedroom, and they paid *her*, they were all the same. If it wasn't her money they wanted, it was her body, or her eternal soul.

Bastards, all of them, ready to screw you over at the first chance they got.

Brenda picked the clock off the bedside cabinet and peered at its glowing figures.

5:06 AM

She put the clock back and started chewing on a nail. Not much chance of her getting back to sleep now. Once she was awake, that was it, she was awake for hours. That was always the problem with having Peter around. He'd wake up in the night, having a nightmare, or crying because he'd wet the bed. And he'd wake Brenda up, bloody stupid kid.

Why did he have to do that? He was too old to be scared of the dark anymore, and he bloody well knew where the clean sheets were kept, didn't he? It was about time he started looking after himself a bit more, was what she'd tell him.

But no, the stupid little boy insisted on waking her up, wanting her to tell him that there weren't any monsters lurking in the wardrobe, or under the bed. Wanting her to change his sheets for clean, dry ones.

Brenda picked up a packet of cigarettes off her bedside cabinet and pulled one out. No point in even trying to get back to sleep now. She lit the cigarette and took a deep drag, savouring that first giddy moment as the nicotine hit her bloodstream.

Bloody stupid Peter, most probably just like his bloody father, whoever the hell he was. What the hell did he think he was playing at? Him and that other boy, Jacob, they were hiding out somewhere, playing at being silly buggers. None of this stupid fuss with the police had been necessary, but Laura, she had to go and get them involved.

Her being Tom Mills' wife, and all. You'd have thought when you were married to the Slaughterhouse Mob, the police would be the last people you'd call. But no, Laura had to go and get them looking for the kids, creating a bloody storm in a teacup if you asked Brenda, and now here she was, Public Enemy Number One, according to the papers.

Oh yes, she knew what the police thought of her, and she'd read the newspapers, all those bloody editors sitting in their swanky London offices, ranting on about what an unfit mother she was. What was it *The Daily Mail* had said about her? 'Brenda Marsden is a shabby symbol of the state of our once proud nation', or some such bloody shit.

All a load of bloody bollocks, that's what it was.

Brenda took another drag on her cigarette, and then held her breath. Listening.

For a moment her chest had contracted, her stomach tightened, the oppressive fear from her nightmare sweeping over her once more. It was her imagination, it must have been. The wind, perhaps, playing tricks with her hearing, with her nerves.

Because, surely she couldn't have heard Peter calling for her from his bedroom?

Brenda sat perfectly still in the bed, smoke from the cigarette, held between two fingers, drifting past her face.

Nothing, just the empty silence of the house.

God, this house can be bloody lonely at night, she thought. Although the boy had been nothing but a bloody nuisance and a drain on her pocket ever since he came along, at least he was a bit of company sometimes. Like in the evenings, when her men friends were back home with their wives, it was nice to have the lad around then.

He had a right tongue on him, that was for sure, giving her cheek so much she sometimes couldn't help but give him a slap. It was for his own good, that mouth of his was going to get him into trouble one day. But he could be funny, too. Some of the stories he told her, making them up on the spot like that, he'd have her crying with laughter by the end.

Bloody hell, Brenda, the way you're going on, anybody'd think you were missing the little sod.

She took another drag on her cigarette.

Brenda jumped as she heard a clatter from outside, and bottles rolling along the drive.

Cats, she thought, as her heart picked up its galloping pace again. *That's all, just the bloody cats.*

A long, grey column of ash had grown on Brenda's cigarette, threatening to collapse onto her duvet. She tapped it into the ashtray, the one with the portrait of Elvis in the base. Her first husband had been an obsessive fan of Elvis, and tortured Brenda by playing his records all day long. He'd hated that ashtray, said she shouldn't be stubbing her cigarettes out in the King's face.

Bloody hell, he couldn't even see that's why she'd bought it in the first place.

And why she still hung onto it all these years later.

Another clatter of rubbish from outside startled Brenda, and she dropped her cigarette on the duvet. She snatched it up, and stubbed it out in the ashtray.

I'm going to kill those bloody cats, she thought, climbing out of the bed. She twitched the curtains aside, and peered through the gap, down into the darkness of her garden. All she could see was her distorted reflection in the glass.

Pulling on her slippers and a faded dressing gown, she headed downstairs. In the kitchen, in a cupboard under the sink, she found a torch. She hadn't used it in years, but when she flicked the switch it gave out a weak, yellow light.

She unlocked the back door, and stepped outside.

Silence.

Brenda swung the torch around in a slow arc, past the small, derelict shed, more holes in the roof than there was actual roof, past the overgrown lawn full of weeds, and the engine block left behind by one of her boyfriends. He'd promised to come back for it, but Brenda had given up expecting him.

And there, on the flagstone patio, was her dustbin, lying on its side, the contents strewn behind it in a wide arc.

Not a sign of cats anywhere.

Brenda turned back to go inside.

I'll pick all the rubbish up later.

The skin on her neck and arms goose pimpled as she heard the slow shuffle of footsteps in the dark. She swung the torch back around, her other hand clutching at her dressing gown. There was no one in the garden, no one that she could see at least.

But she had heard something.

"Who's there?" she said.

Another sound, like someone laboriously dragging a heavy weight, inch by painful inch, along the ground.

Whoever, whatever, was making that noise, they were coming closer.

Brenda stepped back, her heel catching on the lip of the doorstep. She began to fall, tipping backwards. Her arms shot out and began pinwheeling around as she tried to regain her balance, or grab onto the door frame. The light from the torch swung around and around, casting crazy, kaleidoscopic shadows across the walls, transforming the kitchen into a lunatic funfair ride from a black and white horror movie.

Brenda fell on her bottom, and the shock sent the torch flying from her hand and skidding across the kitchen floor. The bulb flickered wildly, and then died, plunging her into darkness.

"Oh no, oh no, no, no, nonononoonooo . . .!"

She scrabbled around on the floor, disorientated in her terror, trying to find the door. She had to shut the back door before that thing, whatever it was, got inside the house. She swept her hands wildly across the dirty linoleum, until her knuckles smacked against the edge of the doorstep.

Crying out in pain and fear, Brenda slid her hands up the open door until she found the handle, all the time expecting her wrist to be seized by the clawed, deformed hand of a nightmarish monster from the depths of hell. Crying with relief, she pulled at the door and slammed it shut, her shaking fingers finding the key and twisting it locked.

Something heavy and ponderous thumped against the door, and Brenda screamed. There was another thump, and then the slap of something flat and wet, against the glass. Brenda pulled herself backwards, her bottom sliding along the floor, staring wide eyed at her back door. There was little to see, other than vague shadows, and the suggestion of movement, in the darkness.

She screamed again when she hit her head against the table. Whatever was outside seemed agitated by her scream, and began pawing at her back door. Brenda turned over, reaching out to get on her hands and knees, when she found the torch. She closed her hand around it and picked it up.

The torch flickered into life again, the beam suddenly growing steadier.

As if pulled by an outside force, unable to command her body to stop, she slowly turned around, casting the light on her back door.

A white face was pressed against the window in the upper half of the door, blood from a gash in the cheek smeared against the glass in a long, wide streak. Round eyes stared at her, the pupils so big and black, they seemed to take up the whole of the eye sockets. On either side of the ghastly head, two hands were pushed against the glass, the fingers splayed out.

There was a squeaking sound as it shifted position slightly, leaving more bloody smears across the window. It opened its mouth, and pressed a red, pointed tongue against the glass, and started licking at the blood.

Brenda screamed.

That thing outside was her Peter.

She screamed and screamed, and dropped the torch from nerveless fingers. It hit the floor, the bulb giving up again, and leaving her in darkness once more.

Sobbing hysterically, Brenda managed to start crawling away from the back door, into the hall and then up the stairs.

Outside, the lifeless thing that used to be her son, continued licking frantically at its own blood smeared across the window pane.

it's all bullshit

When Joe Coffin woke up, his eyes were full of grit, and his head felt like somebody had punched a metal spike through it.

There were no curtains in the flat, and the morning sky was a clear, sharp edged blue. Coffin dragged himself out of bed, and rummaged through his holdall for some clean clothes, squinting in the sunlight. He pulled on a T-shirt and jeans.

In the bathroom he splashed cold water over his face. He ran his tongue over his teeth. They felt fuzzy, sticky. Yesterday he had meant to buy a toothbrush and toothpaste. He walked into the kitchen and found the whisky bottle. He rinsed a small amount of whisky around his mouth, before swallowing it.

The clock on the kitchen wall said the time was ten past eight. He would have liked to have slept in for longer, but the sunshine had prodded him awake. He prowled around the flat, in and out of the bedroom, bathroom, kitchen and living room. Not sure what he was looking for. Not sure he was looking for anything.

He headed downstairs and outside, the cold morning air like a slap in the face, bringing him fully awake. The street was busy with rush hour traffic, the pavement with mothers taking their children to school. Coffin walked to the corner shop. He began scanning the newspaper headlines, and stopped.

Coffin picked up the newspaper and unfolded it, so that he could read the entire headline.

BRUTAL GANGLAND MURDER IN CITY

Coffin gripped the newspaper, his fingers tightening around the edges, scrunching the paper into his palms.

He scanned through the story, looking for any details about the two kids, about any possible connection the police were looking at in relation to his family's murders. As usual, the police were remaining tight lipped.

"Hey, are you buying that paper, or not? This isn't a library, you know!"

Coffin looked up from the newspaper, at the shopkeeper, standing behind his counter, rolls of fat stretching at his shirt. Greasy hair, pasty skin, full, wet lips, he looked to Coffin like someone who deserved a good kicking. Coffin could imagine doing that, saw himself taking out all his grief and misery, all his anger, on this piece of shit.

The man, as though reading Coffin's intentions in his eyes, took a step back, his eyes widening.

Coffin walked over to the counter, and leaned on it, upsetting a display of lottery tickets, which crashed to the floor.

"What did you say?"

The man backed up again, into shelves of cigarette packets. He was shaking so bad he upset the displays, and the packets began falling, bouncing off his shoulders and his huge stomach.

"I just asked if you were buying the paper, that's all."

Coffin leaned over the counter, grabbed the shopkeeper by the collar, and hauled him forward until their faces were only inches apart.

The fat man clutched at Coffin's wrists, tried to pull himself free. He might as well have been trying to prise open a locked door with his fingers.

Coffin stared into his wide, frightened eyes. Tears were gathering on the lids, quivering and ready to spill down his cheeks. Coffin grabbed the man's face in one hand, squeezing his cheeks together, so that his lips stuck out in a comical pout.

How easy it would be to simply keep on squeezing, until he felt the bones of the skull cave in beneath the pressure, heard the crack of bone just before the man began screaming.

The bell over the shop door tinged.

Coffin let go, and the man staggered and fell back, on his bottom. Breathing tortuously, his hands massaging his face, the shopkeeper stared up at Coffin. He looked about ready to burst into tears.

Coffin picked up his newspaper and walked outside.

As he walked, he continued reading. There was no mention of the girl that Coffin had told to get out. He regretted letting her go. If she went to the police, she could easily identify him. Maybe she had already gone, and the police were keeping quiet.

No, Coffin couldn't figure that one. The cops would have said they were pursuing an important lead, or some bullshit like that. They had to say something to justify their existence.

It bothered him about those two kids, though. Coffin never would have named them as the killers. They didn't fit the picture in his head. Coffin should never have listened to Tom Mills, he should have trusted his instinct. He thought about what Craggs had said, about Chinese whispers, about Tom looking after Coffin's interests while he was in jail.

Here was another detail that bothered him. Joe Coffin and Tom Mills had never had much time for each other before now. What Coffin had ended up hating the most about his divorce from Laura was that she went on to marry Tom Mills. The guy was a complete waste of space, always had been. What had compelled Laura to hook up with him was beyond Coffin's ability to reason.

The divorce with Laura had been amicable, and they remained friends. So, Coffin had kept out of the way, and not criticised Laura for her choice of partner. If she wanted to marry him, that was up to her. But then Jacob arrived, and Coffin saw a change for the worse in Tom, an aggressive streak he had never displayed before. It was like he suddenly had this monkey on his back, nipping and scratching at him, whispering in his ear, goading him on to increasingly nasty outbursts.

Coffin had been ready to rip Tom's arms off when he found out about the assault on Laura. But Craggs had forbidden him from interfering, had calmed him down, saying he would deal with it.

Mortimer Craggs insisted on visiting Laura, taking Tom with him. Coffin came along, too, giving Tom the dead eye the whole time. Tom begged for Laura's forgiveness, cried his eyes out in front of everyone.

Coffin knew it was all bullshit. Tom didn't care what Laura thought, didn't give a shit about the bruises on her face, the stitches in the back of her head. The dramatic display of regret was for Mortimer Craggs, and nobody else.

Craggs didn't like it when the organisation that was the Slaughterhouse Mob didn't run as smoothly as it ought. Craggs had founded the Slaughterhouse Mob, and been its leader ever since. He demanded fierce loyalty from every member of the Mob, and that included the wives.

Which meant, that once Tom Mills had finished his desperate pleading for forgiveness, Laura had little choice other than to accept his apology, and take him back. Coffin had already told her that she shouldn't take him back, and that he would support her, talk Craggs round.

But Laura took Tom back, and it wasn't that big a surprise, really. Coffin felt bad for Laura, even more so for the boy, Jacob. He wasn't going to let Tom hurt them again.

And Tom knew that.

But now, here he was, acting like Coffin's best friend. It didn't sit easy with Coffin.

Not at all.

Coffin read the rest of the story.

When he'd finished, he folded the newspaper up, and stuffed it into a bin.

He stopped at a florists, and bought some lilies.

Then he began the walk to the churchyard, where Steffanie and Michael were buried.

* * *

Tom Mills gripped the edge of the white toilet bowl, and threw up. He wiped a trembling arm over his forehead slick with sweat, and spat into the toilet. Sitting down on the bathroom floor, his back against the bath, he tore some paper off the toilet roll and dabbed at his lips. His head was pounding, and the morning light hurt the back of his eyes.

Reaching up to flush the toilet, Tom noticed his hand was black. He looked at his other hand. It was black too. He held both hands up in front of his face. His palms looked like a negative image, the tracery of fine lines running across the surface standing out in white against the black.

There were black smudges where he had been gripping the toilet bowl, and when he looked up he saw a black hand print on the wall by the bathroom door.

What the hell was going on?

Tom lifted a shaky hand to his nose and sniffed cautiously. The palm of his hand smelt of soil.

Tom groaned and closed his eyes as he remembered finding the open grave last night. There were several large gaps in his recollection of events, fragments of memory only. But he remembered shovelling the dirt back into the grave with his bare hands.

And he remembered sobbing helplessly while he gathered up the mounds of earth, and pushed them over the edges of the grave.

Tom struggled to his feet and gazed at his reflection in the bathroom mirror. His face was smudged with black, and so was his shirt and trousers. He had no memory of how he got home, but he must have crawled straight into bed fully dressed. Still wearing his shoes.

He opened the bathroom window and looked outside. The car was parked at an angle, half on the drive and half on the front lawn. But there was no sign that he could see, of any damage to the car. Surely, if he had been involved in an accident last night, he would have known about it by now?

Wearily, Tom put the plug in the bath and turned on the hot water tap.

The room began spinning, another wave of nausea building inside his stomach. Tom sat down on the floor, beside the toilet. His head ached, along with his legs and arms and back.

Slowly, he began the laborious job of untying his shoelaces. He refused to think about last night, not yet at least. After a long soak in the bath he would go back to bed, get some more sleep.

And then, maybe then, he could try and think about what he had seen.

* * *

Joe Coffin stood beneath the shade of a massive Oak tree. Brown leaves floated gently to the ground all around him. From where he stood, Coffin had a clear view of the police, their vans and forensic crews, and the yellow scene of crime tape.

Every now and then someone would stop, crane their necks to try and take a look, maybe see if there was a body still there. They were quickly moved on by a policeman. A reporter stood a little way off, talking into his mobile.

Coffin still held the lilies, forgotten, by his side. He'd been on his way to the graveyard when he saw the police vans, the crowd of onlookers. It didn't take long to find out what was going on. A tramp had been found early this morning, the cold body lying half on, half off a park bench, his throat ripped open in a savage attack.

And now Coffin didn't feel like going to the graveyard. Not if the murderer of his wife and son was still out there, still killing people.

At the sound of rustling behind him, Coffin turned around. A tramp, hunched up like a question mark, shuffled through the leaves towards him. As the beggar approached, Coffin saw long, white hair cascading from beneath an oversized deerstalker, and realised he was looking at an old woman. She wore a large, tattered winter coat, several skirts, and a huge pair of boots. Behind her she was dragging a battered shopping bag on wheels.

She stopped beside Coffin and peered up at him.

"I haven't got any money," Coffin said, and turned his attention back to the crime scene in the distance.

The old woman huffed, and spat a gob of yellow phlegm on the ground. "Did I ask you for any money?"

"No, I don't suppose you did," Coffin said.

"Well then, what gives you the right to assume that I walked over here just to ask you for some spare change?"

"I apologise," Coffin replied.

"That's all right then," the old woman said. "Now, what's so interesting to you about all the fuss they're making over there?"

Coffin sighed. Prison and life on the outside were sometimes very similar. Wherever he was, there always seemed to be somebody interested in his business.

"I don't mean to be rude, old lady, but this is none of your business."

"Seems it ought not to be any of your business either, otherwise why would you be skulking around under the shade of this tree, instead of up there talking to those officers?"

Coffin looked down at the old lady again. Even standing straight, she would still be tiny. Because of his size, most people gave Coffin a wide berth. But this little old woman seemed to have no fear of him at all.

"What about you?" he said. "What business is this of yours?"

"I knew old Alfred, long before he took to sleeping on that park bench, that's what business it is of mine."

"I'm sorry," Coffin said. "He was your friend."

The old woman stuffed a hand inside her jacket and scratched. "Wouldn't say we were friends, necessarily, more like passing acquaintances."

"How long had you known him?"

"Oh, we'd been bumping into each other on and off for the last twenty years or so, I reckon. Used to be that we'd see each other in the homeless shelters, but in later years we seem to have spent more time sleeping rough, coming across one another in the backstreets, or heading for the same park bench after sunset."

"Sounds like a hard life," Coffin said, turning his attention to the crime scene once more.

"Well, maybe," she said. "But I had a home once, and a husband, and money, and it seems to me that being homeless is just a different kind of hard life to not being homeless."

"You could be right."

"Take that poor woman and her boy got murdered, in their own home. That's no different to Alf getting his throat cut open out here, in the open, now is it?"

"I suppose not," Coffin said.

"It were like a fiend from Hell," the old lady said.

"What?" Coffin snapped his attention back to her. "Did you see the attack?"

She shook her head. "No, but I know someone who did." She scrunched up her face. "Used to know his name once, but it escapes me now."

Coffin got down on one knee, like an adult in front of a child, so they could talk on the same level. "What did your friend see, did he tell you?"

The old lady pushed a few wisps white of hair out of her face. "He were down here, right where we are standing now. Said he was on his way up to the bench, could see Alf laid out on it already, could hear him snoring clear all the way over here."

She fell silent, and Coffin waited. Eventually, he said, "And then what happened?"

"Don't rightly know. My friend, he drinks a lot, and he's seen a few things over the years that I know aren't right. But this time, maybe . . ."

"Maybe what?"

"Said he saw a dark shape drop from the tree over the bench. A shadow, fell on Alf, and the next thing he knew, Alf is screaming and thrashing, and fighting at this shadow, and before my friend could even think about what to do next, Alf's screams had turned into gurgles, and he stopped fighting, and lay still."

"And what did this . . . shadow, do next?"

"It started feeding on Alf, and my friend doesn't know any more, because he turned and ran, and as far as I know, he's begging for enough change today that he can buy himself a bus ticket and catch the first bus out of here."

"Do you believe him?" Coffin asked.

"No. Today's Friday, and on Friday nights, there's some church folk set up a soup kitchen down at the market, and you get a hot cup of tea, soup and a bread roll. He'll be there."

"I meant, do you believe him about what he saw, about how Alf got killed?"

"I don't know," the old lady said, quietly. "I've never had cause to believe any of his crazy stories before, but this time . . . this time I just don't know."

Coffin stood up, looked back at the police on the brow of the hill, then back down at the old lady.

"Here, have these" he said, handing her the lilies, and turned and walked away.

emma visits
the bathroom

Emma yelped as a boy on a BMX shot past, narrowly missing her. She stared at his back as he raced down the street, laughing.

Shouldn't he be in school? Today was a Friday, and still term time as far as she could remember.

But then what did she care?

Children had never interested Emma. The thought of another life form growing inside her body, swelling her belly until it grew so big it had to be removed, screaming and covered in filth, was repulsive enough. And then there were the shitty nappies, the vomit, the sleepless nights, the endless feeding, and the responsibility . . . Dear God, why would anybody want to do that?

She'd been clear with Nick right from the start, no kids. Kids just got in the way, and she had her career to think about. Emma had mapped out her life plan whilst still a teenager. First there was journalism school, and then a job on any old local rag, just to get her foot in the door. After gaining some experience, and several contacts within the industry, the next stage of her plan involved getting the scoop on a major story. Then, if the story was big enough, she could quit journalism to write a book about her sensational part in this major expose. Using her earnings from book sales, and her fame as an investigative journalist, she then planned to follow her ultimate dream of writing novels for a living.

And starting a family did not feature anywhere in that plan. Neither did having a relationship, if she was honest, but sometimes life took you on a different course. Still, the relationship with Nick changed nothing, and if he wasn't happy with the plan, he knew where the door was.

At thirty-two years of age, Emma was pleased with how her plan had worked out so far. It had taken her a little longer than expected, and she had hoped to have been working on one of the national newspapers by now. But still, for a local newspaper, the *Birmingham Herald* was pretty big.

Emma had hoped that Steffanie Coffin was going to be her ticket to that career making exclusive. They had only met three times, still at the point of sizing each other up, working out the deal. That last time they met, Steffanie had brought her little boy with her. And she had been jittery, convinced that someone was onto her.

They met in a country pub, The Fifth Lock, on the bank of a canal. As far away from any of the local haunts of the Slaughterhouse Mob as they could get. Emma had arrived early for their meeting. She parked her rusty, battered Ford Fiesta in a corner of the small, dusty car park, and waited for Steffanie to arrive. Twenty minutes later, Steffanie's sleek BMW pulled into the car park. Emma watched as Steffanie dragged the buggy out of the gleaming BMW, along with a bulging mamas & papas rucksack, a bag with toys in, and finally the little boy, crying and waving his fists.

Emma had waited until she saw Steffanie walk inside the pub, and then she had waited another fifteen minutes, sitting in her car, watching out for anybody suspicious looking, or familiar to her from photographs of the Slaughterhouse Mob gang members.

Finally she walked inside the cool, darkened pub, and found Steffanie sitting in a corner, a large glass of red wine on the table.

The boy had been in his buggy, and Steffanie had spent their whole time together constantly pushing the buggy back and forth, as though trying to lull the child to sleep. But even Emma, with her limited knowledge of children, could see the boy was too big for the buggy, too old be strapped in and sent to sleep.

He yanked at the straps, his fingers fumbling with the clips, his fine motor skills not yet developed enough to be able to undo them. Steffanie had given him books, and sweets, and brightly coloured plastic toys to shake and bang, or twist and chew.

The boy had thrown everything on the floor, except the sweets, which kept him quiet until he had eaten them all, his lips turned bright orange. He cried and yelled and struggled and kicked, until Steffanie ignored him, but still kept pushing the buggy, up and down, up and down.

Emma ordered a cafetiere of coffee, and took the opportunity to examine Steffanie whilst she was busy fussing with the boy. Emma knew all about Steffanie's career as a pole dancer, and had to admit she looked the part. Tall and slim, perfectly proportioned chest, tanned, and that shock of gorgeous red hair, all added up to the kind of girl that terrified Emma when she was at school.

"I've got something for you," Steffanie said, leaving the boy alone to struggle and cry.

Emma had been plunging her cafetiere, and stopped. "Really?"

Steffanie took a long swallow of her wine, perfectly manicured fingers holding the glass. "No, nothing you can use, but something to show you I'm serious, that I do have the goods."

Emma finished plunging her cafetiere, and poured the black coffee into her cup. She took her time, sipping at the coffee. It was good, strong and full bodied, just the way she liked it.

"What is it then?" she said, finally. "Show me what you've got and we can talk some more."

Steffanie opened up the rucksack and pulled out a pack of baby wipes. The pack had a seal on the top, already open, to pull out individual wipes. Steffanie ripped open the entire plastic pack and dumped the wet baby wipes on the table. She leafed through the wipes until she found a square piece of clingfilm, with a sheet of folded paper inside, which she pushed across the table.

Emma wondered how long it had taken Steffanie to insert that piece of paper inside the folds of the baby wipes, through that small hole in the top.

Emma peeled the clingfilm apart and unfolded the paper. It was a photo. Printed off a home printer. It looked like a still from a surveillance camera, a wide angle view of an office, with a man sitting at a desk, holding a telephone to his ear.

"Is that Terry Wu?" Emma said.

Steffanie picked a rattle off the floor and handed it to the boy. He threw it at her.

"Yes," she said. "Two minutes after that, Terry was murdered. I can get you a photo of that, too."

Emma raised her eyebrows. "Are you fucking serious?" She put a hand to her mouth, glancing at the boy. "Oh, shit, sorry about that."

"Don't worry about it, he's heard worse," Steffanie said. "And yes, I'm serious."

"And you've got a photo of Terry being murdered?"

"Better than that, I've got the whole thing on video. Complete with a perfectly clear view of the murderer."

Emma leaned forward, her stomach suddenly doing summersaults. "Who's on the video, Steffanie? Who pulled the trigger?"

"Uh uh," Steffanie said, snatching the blurry photograph of Terry Wu from Emma's hand. "You don't get no more until we've got a deal."

Steffanie pulled a gold lighter from the pocket on the rucksack, and flicked it open. She touched the flame to the print, the paper quickly catching fire, swallowing the photograph in a bright yellow flame. Steffanie stuffed the burning paper into her empty wine glass, jabbing at it with her perfectly manicured fingers, until there was nothing but curled, blackened paper left.

The pub landlady, all wrinkles and makeup, rushed over.

"What's going on? Is everything all right?"

"Sorry about that, a little accident with my lighter."

"Smoking's not allowed in here, you know. If you want to smoke, you'll have to sit outside, in the beer garden."

"No thank you," Steffanie replied. She slid the wine glass, the blackened paper curled up inside, across the table. "Could I have another red wine, please? And a fresh glass."

"You're pretty damn sure of yourself, aren't you?" Emma said, as the old lady returned to the bar, the ruined wine glass in hand.

"Sure enough to know I want out of the life," Steffanie said.

"Why?" Emma said. "Joe gets out of jail in another three months, will you be waiting for him? Or is it him you're getting away from?"

Steffanie levelled her cool gaze at Emma. "I didn't agree to meet you, just so I could answer your questions. Now why don't you stop acting like a silly little girl, pretending to be a journalist, and we can talk about the deal?"

"You think I'm pretending, here?" Emma drew herself up a little straighter, tried to ignore that feeling of intimidation from her school years.

"I'm thinking you're awfully young to be hanging with the big boys and girls. Shouldn't you still be at home with mummy, playing dress up?"

Emma leaned across the table, her voice low. "Fuck you, Steffanie. You want, we can finish this right here and now, and you can waste another few weeks persuading another newspaper to pay you for giving them the scoop that will bring down Craggs and his mob. That is, if you actually have anything. So far, you've shown me shit."

"Calm down, little girl," Steffanie said. "I'm here, aren't I?"

They fell silent as the landlady returned, with a fresh glass of wine for Steffanie.

"Don't usually do table service here," the old lady said. "Customers usually come to the bar and order their drinks there."

"I appreciate you taking the trouble to accommodate me," Steffanie replied.

The landlady left, the look on her face saying she still wasn't sure she had made her point.

"My editor's getting itchy," Emma said. "If we're going ahead with this story, we need to get moving. Which means it's down to you, telling us your story, bringing us the evidence. Who pulled the trigger, Steffanie?"

"We haven't discussed payment yet."

"Are you kidding me? We've done nothing but discuss the fucking money! Who pulled the trigger?"

Steffanie said nothing, holding Emma in her cool, level gaze.

"Seriously, Steffanie, I'm about ready to call this whole thing off. You need to give us something before we take it any further." Emma leaned forward, staring at Steffanie. "Who pulled the fucking trigger?"

Steffanie sighed. "It was Joe."

"Joe Coffin? Your fucking husband?"

Michael let out a cry, and Steffanie bent down to see to him, pushing more sweets into his fumbling hands.

Emma sat back in her chair. Joe Coffin murdered Terry Wu. A low flicker of excitement burst to life in the pit of her stomach. Finally, she was on the cusp of that big, career making story. She'd have to be careful how she handled this, especially with Nick. Maybe take the evidence to the police the morning the story was due to break in the newspaper. Of course she had to give them a heads up, but not too much. This was her story, and she was going to break it how she wanted.

"All right, let's talk money," she said.

Steffanie raised an eyebrow. "And?"

"And, Karl says we can go up to £250,000, dependent on you giving us what you've promised."

"Is that all?"

"Holy fuck, Steffanie, get a grip. That kind of money, a national newspaper pays for a celebrity to dish the dirt. You're hardly big news outside of the Midlands, and even here you're more in the notorious class than the celebrity status."

"With what I've got, you'll be bringing down the biggest extortion and drug running gang in the country. I would have thought—"

"Nobody gives a shit what you think," Emma snapped. "What everybody else will be thinking is, if that high class hooker's so concerned with bringing down the Slaughterhouse Mob, why the fuck didn't she go straight to the police?"

Anger flared briefly across Steffanie's face, and for a moment that childhood fear filled Emma's chest again.

I've gone too far, she thought.

The mask slipped back into place, Steffanie's face regaining its perfect composure. "I suppose that payment will have to do then."

Emma sat back and took a deep breath. "Good, now we're getting somewhere."

She picked up her cup and took a sip of the coffee. She grimaced. As much as she loved coffee, she hated cold coffee.

"Next time we meet," Emma said, "you bring all the evidence you have. Everything. And you tell me the whole story, too. We can't dick about like this anymore. The longer we wait, the more dangerous it gets."

Steffanie smiled, and sipped her wine. The smile wasn't warm, or comforting, or pleasant. It was cold and cruel, and patronising. "You have no idea how much danger I am in. And you, too."

"Like I said, the sooner we get this done, the better. How are you going to get the video of Terry Wu's murder to us?"

"Everything I have, including the footage of the murder, and rock solid evidence linking Craggs to extortion, drug dealing, the smuggling of illegal immigrants into the country, *everything*, is on a USB stick. I'll give it to you soon, but we still need to discuss the terms of the payment."

Steffanie stood up, started gathering the toys and baby paraphernalia together.

"What are you doing?" Emma said.

Steffanie picked up her glass and drained the rest of the wine. "I have to go. I'll be in touch."

She wheeled the buggy around and pushed it through the pub. Emma watched as she manoeuvred the buggy outside, the door slamming shut behind her.

"Don't mention it," Emma said, to the empty chair. "I'm perfectly happy to pick up the bill. No need to thank me, no need at all. *Fuck!*"

* * *

Three days later, Emma got the news that Steffanie and Michael had been murdered. A numb dismay had been her only emotion.

The following morning, she climbed out of bed, made herself a coffee, and then sat in her kitchen the rest of the day, crying. The guilt had been overpowering, debilitating. It had taken several calls from her editor, and a personal visit, before she started the process of coming to terms with what had happened, and her possible role in it.

It was the little boy's death that hit her most. Steffanie had lived the life, she was going out one way or another. Maybe lung cancer, or her liver packing up, or maybe a good beating from her husband, or a lover. But that little boy, how old had he been? Two, three maybe?

The BMX boy had long since disappeared from her line of view, but still Emma stared after him, lost in her thoughts.

She had a feeling that Michael Coffin was going to haunt her waking, and sleeping, hours for many years to come.

Emma opened the boot of her car and grabbed a camera, hooking the strap over her shoulder. Jonny, the young, long haired staff photographer, had been called out on another job. That was fine with Emma, she could take a photograph just as well as the staff photographers, as far as she was concerned. The D4 might be bigger, shinier and have more buttons and dials than her own compact camera, but what was the difference? You pointed the lens at your subject and pushed a button.

What was the big deal?

Emma rested her backside against her car, and looked at the house. An interview with Laura Mills wasn't going to be easy, even though she had agreed to it. Another story about her missing child, keeping him alive in the public consciousness, couldn't hurt, and might even do some good. Laura knew that. She was a mother, she wanted her boy home, and would do anything to achieve that.

But still, it was going to be an emotionally difficult interview.

And what was with the car parked on the driveway? Or, rather, the car parked at an angle, half on the drive and half on the lawn, with the long scratch running down the driver's side. Looked like someone had been trying to park it, and then abandoned it. At some point in the process of trying to park, whoever had been driving had hit the second car parked on the same drive. The passenger door was crumpled in, just at the point where the other car was facing it. Looked like someone had been having a bad day.

Or night.

Emma walked up to the front door and rang the doorbell. Laura answered almost immediately.

Her eyes were red, and her face blotchy. Had she been crying? Had she even managed to get any sleep since Jacob and Peter disappeared?

Emma stuck out her hand. "Hi, I'm Emma from the *Birmingham Herald*, we spoke on the phone yesterday."

Laura looked at Emma's hand as though it might bite her. Eventually she shook, briefly, before snatching her hand back. Her movements were jerky, quick, like she was operated by tightly coiled springs.

"I suppose you want to come in," she said, her voice flat, like she had made a statement, rather than asked a question.

"I think it would be easier on you if we talked inside, yes," Emma said.

Laura made no move to let her in the house. "What's the camera for?"

"Oh, well, if you don't mind, of course, we thought, my editor and I thought, that it might be a good idea if we got a photograph of you, and maybe your husband as well, if he's at home right now, that is, to go with the interview."

Fuck! Emma thought. *Get a grip on yourself, you sound like a giddy teenager asking a girl out on a date.*

"Yes, Tom is at home," Laura replied, her voice a monotone. "He came home late last night, he's having a bath right now."

"Oh good, he'll look nice for the photograph, then."

Shit, did I just say that? Emma cringed inwardly.

Laura regarded Emma for a few seconds more, her eyes dull and red rimmed, until she finally stepped back and let Emma inside.

Emma had expected the house to be in a state of chaos, the demands of normal life, such as tidying and cleaning, put on hold for the moment. All of Laura's energy would be focused on finding her missing son, surely? Emma had half expected Laura to be out when she called, scouring the streets, knocking on doors, pinning missing persons posters up all over town.

But no, here Laura stood, like an estate agent in a brand new house, ready to give Emma the tour. The air smelt of polish, the hall carpet looked freshly vacuumed, the house just seemed to radiate cleanliness and order.

And, come to think of it, despite the red rimmed eyes, Laura looked smart and well presented, too. Was this all for Emma's benefit? Or was this her way of coping with the stress?

"Would you like a coffee?" Laura said.

"Yes, please," Emma replied.

She followed Laura into the kitchen. The smell of cleaning spray hung in the air. The hob sparkled, looking like it had just been installed, and all the surfaces were clean and free of clutter.

"You have a lovely house," Emma said, and mentally kicked herself. Was now the right time to be making small talk?

"It's all right," Laura said, switching the kettle on.

Emma put the camera down on the table and pulled out her notebook. Maybe a coffee had been a bad idea. Best just to get the interview and the photograph and then go. She wasn't even sure she wanted to hang around until Tom Mills had finished having a bath. From what she'd heard so far, he hadn't been that bothered about his missing son.

"Do you mind if I take some photos of you?" Emma said. "The natural ones sometimes work so much better than posed shots."

"Whatever you think's best," Laura replied.

Emma switched the camera on.

It's like she's given up. Jacob's been missing three days now, and she's started reconciling herself to the fact that she's never going to see him again. Like she's decided he's already dead.

Emma lifted the camera and composed a shot through the viewfinder. Laura stared vacantly into the camera.

This is good, Emma thought. *Karl might run with this one on the front page.*

"What the hell's going on?"

Emma lowered the camera.

Tom Mills had walked into the kitchen, wearing a dressing gown, hair damp and mussed up, skin red from sitting too long in a hot bath.

Emma stuck out her hand. "Hi, I'm Emma from the *Birmingham Herald*, I'm here to do a story on Jacob."

"Fuck off," Tom growled.

He pushed past her and opened a cupboard, rifling through it until he found a box of matches.

"What did you say?" Emma said.

"You heard me." Tom pulled a pack of cigarettes out of his dressing gown pocket, and started ripping the cellophane off. His hands were shaking. "I told you to fuck off, we don't need no fucking reporters round here."

He finally managed to extricate a cigarette from the pack, and put it in his mouth. His hands were shaking so bad he used up two matches lighting the cigarette. Emma noticed his dirty fingernails, wondered why he hadn't scrubbed them clean while he was sitting in the bath.

But they were more than just dirty, they were black. What had he been doing that got his hands so filthy, it left black crescents of dirt along the ends of his nails even after a bath?

"What are you fucking staring at?" he snapped, blowing a cloud of smoke towards her.

"Sorry," Emma said. "I'll leave."

"Good fucking riddance." Tom pushed past her again, and out of the kitchen.

"I'm sorry about that," Laura said, her voice slow, and quiet. "He's worried about Jacob."

"Yeah, I can imagine," Emma replied. "Maybe if we went somewhere, I could buy you a coffee, and we could talk?"

Laura shook her head. "No, I need to stay here. I'll see you to the door."

They stepped back into the hall and Emma glanced up the stairs. On the left hand side, about a quarter of the way up, was a black hand print. Further up the stairs was another one, slightly smudged, but just as filthy as the last.

Emma smiled bashfully. "Um, I'm sorry to ask, but would you mind if I used your toilet? I need to pee, and I don't think I'll make it back to the office, if I'm honest."

"No, I don't mind," Laura replied.

Emma walked up the stairs. There was another hand print at the top, and then more along the landing wall, until they reached a bedroom door. Up here there was a trail of dirty footprints on the carpet, too. The vacuum cleaner sat on the landing.

Emma glanced back. Laura had gone back into the kitchen. The stairs carpet was clean. Laura had been vacuuming when Emma knocked on the door.

Covering up for something, maybe? Or someone, more likely.

Emma followed the trail of hand prints to the bedroom and gently pushed the door open. The bed was a tangle of bed sheets, looked like somebody had been thrashing around in their sleep, having some real bad nightmares. The sheets and the covers looked filthy, too.

Emma pulled the door to, and followed the dirty footprints to the bathroom. She opened the door, and was met by moist, warm air. There were more hand prints on the bathroom wall, on the toilet bowl and flush, on the edge of the bath. The inside of the bath was streaked with dirty water marks, and a pile of clothes had been dumped in a corner.

What the hell had Tom been up to last night?

Emma caught her breath. She could hear footsteps on the stairs.

"Hey, you, I thought I told you to get the hell out of my house!"

Emma closed the bathroom door and snapped the lock shut. Whatever had happened last night, she was sure Tom wouldn't be happy that Emma had seen the mess he'd made.

But what was he prepared to do to keep her quiet? He'd never been convicted of anything, but from what she'd heard, Tom Mills was a nasty character. When he found her in here, amongst all these hand prints and the filthy streaks in the bath, would he be ready with an innocent explanation?

Or would it be easier all round if he found a way of keeping her quiet?

Emma flinched as he pounded on the door. "I said I want you out!"

She flushed the toilet and turned on a tap, began washing her hands. "Just a minute, I'm almost done!"

"What are you doing in there?" he shouted. "Come on out, now!"

Fuck, fuck, fuck! He's going to fucking kill you, unless you think of something, quick!

She glanced around the bathroom, looking for a weapon.

Shampoo, soap, shower gel, a pumice stone, a toilet brush.

Fuck, maybe I could tickle him with the toilet brush, and get out whilst he's still lying on the floor giggling helplessly.

More pounding, the door quivering in its frame. "Do I have to kick this door in, and drag you out of there?"

"No, just a sec, I'm almost done, I just need to . . . wait, I think I need to pee again!"

The bathroom window! If she climbed on the bath, hoisted herself up, maybe she could squeeze through the gap.

Emma screamed as the door crashed open. Tom stood in the ruined doorway, fists clenched by his sides, the tendons on his scrawny neck standing out, a pulse throbbing just under his left jaw.

"You stupid bitch," he hissed.

niiinnuuuhh!

It just didn't make sense, no matter how he looked at it. When he'd been in their scuzzy apartment, stinking of unwashed bodies, and sex, it had all seemed so obvious. In the heat of the moment, the need for revenge coursing through his body like electricity, Joe Coffin had been ready to pull the trigger, without asking any more questions.

Hell, even if the police had walked in right then, he couldn't have stopped himself. His wife and his son were dead, and their killers needed to pay the price. Blowing that kid's brains out had been the right thing to do.

That's how it had seemed at the time.

But now? Now, Coffin had more questions than answers. Yesterday he had executed his family's murderers. This morning, less than twenty-four hours later, there had been another 'vampire' killing.

How could that be possible?

A copycat murder?

Not likely. People killed other people in the heat of the moment, with their fists, or a gun, or a knife, or whatever came to hand. And mostly they killed family members, not strangers. Or the murder was sexually motivated.

But ripping somebody's throat out with their teeth?

Coffin pulled his jacket collar up as the rain started falling. The pavement was covered in a blanket of wet leaves, slowly turning to mush. Another month or two and it would be much colder, might even start snowing.

That was when Coffin regretted not driving. He should learn how to drive, get himself a custom built car. Or at the very least get his Fat Boy out of the garage. All this walking from place to place was a pain in the arse.

The thing with those kids, Coffin hadn't been thinking clearly when he took them out. But now he was, and he could see, plain as day, that those two scrawny pieces of shit had been maybe just about capable of picking their noses.

But murder?

No. Absolutely not.

Tom, in his eagerness to give Coffin a get out of jail and welcome home present, had found a likely pair for the killers, but not done his homework.

Coffin should talk to him again, find out where he got his information from. He had to have picked up their names from somewhere. Tom should have waited, let Coffin deal with it himself, when he got out.

Coffin trudged on, deep in his thoughts, and oblivious to the rain pouring down his head and under his turned up collar.

* * *

"Keep away from me!" Emma said.

"You shouldn't have come up here," Tom said. "You should have left, like I told you."

"Yeah, that's always been my problem, I never do what I'm told."

Emma backed up, her bottom hitting the edge of the sink. The tap was still running, the water gurgling down the plughole.

Tom hadn't moved from the doorway, as though he couldn't quite decide what to do next. He looked dreadful, and his Adam's apple kept bobbing up and down, like he was getting ready to throw up.

"You look like shit, Tom," Emma said. Wasn't this what they did in the movies, keep the bad guy talking while trying to figure out how to make an escape? "What happened to your car last night, you seen that scratch down the side?"

"What scratch?" Tom said.

"Oh man, you didn't know? That's one big, deep fucker, all the way down the driver's side. You must have been shitfaced not to have noticed that. And is that Laura's car you drove into? You punched a nice big dent in the passenger door. She's going to go fucking ape when she sees that."

Tom's pinched face seemed to grow even tighter with anger. He took a step towards her. He was making a noise, too, a low growling in the back of his throat.

Shit, Emma thought, *maybe keeping him talking was a bad idea. Maybe I should've just tried kicking him in the balls.*

"Tom, what's going on up there?" It was Laura.

Tom stopped moving. He looked unsure of himself. Like he wanted to kill Emma, but not here, in the house. Not in front of his wife.

"Nothing," he said, his voice hoarse. "Everything's fine. The reporter's just leaving."

Tom stepped out of the way, leaving the doorway free for Emma to walk through.

"Get the fuck out of my house," he whispered. "I see you here again, I'll rip your fucking head off. Understand?"

Emma nodded. As she walked past him, he grabbed her by the wrist and hauled her in close. His breath stank, and he had a blood soaked plaster on his thumb. Emma felt sick, and she turned her face away, so she didn't have to breathe in his foul stench.

"One more thing," he said, and smiled. "I think we can assume our little chat is off the record, yes?"

Emma looked him in the eye. "Go fuck yourself."

She twisted her wrist out of his grip and ran down the stairs. Pushing past Laura, Emma stumbled outside and over to her car. Cold drops of rain hit her in the face. Her hands were shaking as she pulled the key fob out and unlocked the doors. She threw the camera on the back seat, climbed inside, and activated the central locking system.

Emma took a deep breath, and gripped the steering wheel. Raindrops and brown, wet leaves blew across the windscreen. Emma could feel the shakes coming on, as adrenalin coursed through her body.

Just got to let it pass, she thought. *You're safe in the car, but if you drive away now, you'll crash.*

Closing her eyes, still gripping the steering wheel, Emma took a few deep breaths. The shakes began subsiding.

She opened her eyes, and saw Joe Coffin approaching Tom and Laura's house. Although she had seen photographs of him, had heard the stories of his tremendous size, this was the first time she had seen him in the flesh.

The man was *huge*. Paint him green and rip his trouser legs off at the knee, and he'd be the Incredible Hulk.

Coffin cast a curious glance at Emma as he walked past, and then turned up the drive, towards the house. Emma watched as he knocked on the front door, saw Laura open it and show him in, watched as the door closed.

Okay, this looks like it might be interesting.

Emma backed the car up, and round a corner, just out of sight of the house. Switching off the engine, she settled down in the car seat, and waited.

* * *

Coffin held Laura whilst she cried softly, her face buried in his chest. This wasn't how it was supposed to have turned out. Coming here to question Tom on what he knew about Steffanie's murder had been a mistake. In his quest for justice, his eagerness to deal out death on those responsible, Coffin had momentarily forgotten that Jacob and his friend were still missing.

"I thought you had some news," Laura said, her voice muffled against Coffin's T-shirt. "It's silly, I know, but when I saw you, I thought maybe you had found them, or that you knew where they were."

There was a thud from upstairs, the sound of a tap running.

"No, I'm sorry." Coffin stroked Laura's hair, like he used to do, years ago. "You haven't heard any more from the police?"

"No." Laura wiped at her eyes. "They want me and Tom to do a news conference today, appeal for witnesses, ask the public for help."

"What about the other boy's mother?"

Coffin thought he heard a small, bitter laugh.

"Brenda?" Laura said. "No, the police want to minimize her exposure in the news. For some reason, they seem to think having a drug addicted, alcoholic prostitute appealing for help on the early evening news might do more harm than good."

Coffin continued stroking Laura's hair. She still had her arms wrapped around him, her head snuggled into his chest. She didn't seem in a hurry to disentangle herself.

There was another thump from upstairs, footsteps over their heads.

"Where's Tom?"

"That's him banging around upstairs. For the first time in his life, I think he might be attempting to clean the bathroom."

"Seriously?"

"Yes, seriously. He's made an awful mess up there, so maybe he feels guilty."

Coffin grunted. "I'm amazed. I've known Tom a lot longer than you, Laura, and I've never known him feel guilty about anything before."

"I know," Laura sighed. "Maybe it was the reporter, I think she shook him up, got him all agitated."

"Is that the girl who was sat outside, in the car?"

"Probably. Is she still there?"

Coffin twisted his head, looked out of the window. "No, she's gone."

They heard Tom walking slowly down the stairs. Coffin pulled Laura away from him, held her gently by the shoulders, and looked down into her eyes.

"Is he hitting you again?" he whispered.

Laura placed her knuckles against her lips, looked down, shook her head.

"Hey, Joe, I thought I heard you down here," Tom said. He was dressed in jeans and a checked shirt. He looked from Laura to Coffin, eyebrows raised. "What's going on?"

"Joe came to see you, Tom," Laura said, wiping at her eyes.

"Yeah?" Tom pulled a squashed cigarette packet out of his back pocket, started patting his other pockets, looking for matches.

"It can wait," Coffin said. "Finding Jacob is the priority right now."

Tom put the cigarette in his mouth, still looking for matches, patting the same pockets all over again.

"You ask me, little bastard's done a runner. He'll be back, whingeing and crying, when he's run out of spending money."

Coffin ignored Tom, looked at Laura again. "He ever done this before, run away?"

"He's not that kind of boy," Laura said. "He's quiet, keeps to himself, doesn't really get into trouble."

Tom walked off, presumably in search of matches.

Laura ran a hand through her hair. "The police have been all through our house, searching through everything, asking questions. They say it's regulation, they do this with every missing persons case, but the way they go about it, you'd think they suspected us of taking Jacob."

"Is that why Tom's on edge? He's like a caged animal."

Laura glanced at the kitchen, where they could hear Tom swearing and banging around, still looking for matches. "He's been nervy for a while now, but he's getting worse at the moment."

Tom returned from the kitchen, sucking on a cigarette.

He let the smoke dribble from his nostrils, and grinned at Coffin. "First one of the day, always hits that sweet spot, know what I mean?"

"Hey, Tom," Coffin said, "Why don't you and me go out for a walk, take a look around, ask a few questions?"

Tom said nothing. The cigarette drooped between his lips, as though he'd forgotten it was there. "Oh, shit."

Coffin spun round, to see what Tom was looking at. Through the window he could see down the street, the leaves blowing along the road, the cars parked on drives, everything quiet.

There was a child staggering along the middle of the road, towards Laura's house. His head seemed to be set at an odd angle, and sometimes he clawed wildly at the air, and then let his arms hang loose by his sides as he continued shambling onwards.

"It's Peter!" Laura whispered.

Coffin yanked the door open and ran down the drive. The boy looked like he was about to fall down at any moment. Coffin bent down and scooped him up, cradling him in his arms. His face and hands were covered in blisters, his skin looked raw and painful to the touch. Peter's head lolled back, and Coffin moaned as he saw the gaping wound in his neck.

The wound looked old, the edges of the torn flesh turning green, and gangrenous. Coffin could see Peter's windpipe, the tendons and the muscles, and he marvelled that the boy was still alive. He carried him up the drive, past Tom's car, and up to the house.

"Call an ambulance!" he shouted.

Laura stared in horror at the boy in Coffin's arms.

Tom pushed past Laura and ran down the drive. Coffin swung around, saw Tom struggling to open the driver's side door, all bashed up from where he had scraped into something.

"Tom?" Coffin said.

Tom ignored him, ran around to the passenger side and climbed into the driving seat.

Tom started up the car and reversed off the drive, spinning the car around, the tyres tearing at grass as he backed up onto the lawn. Coffin watched as Tom revved the engine, struggling to shove the car into first gear.

"Tom, what the hell are you doing?" Coffin roared.

The car lurched off the lawn, and sped erratically down the road, wheels squealing as Tom took the corner at speed, and disappeared from view.

As he turned back to the house, Coffin saw another car pulling out of a side street, and follow Tom's car.

Inside, Laura was on the telephone. Coffin laid the boy down on the settee, and knelt down beside him. Peter's eyes were glassy, unfocused, and Coffin wasn't sure he would live long enough for the paramedics to arrive. And his body had felt so very cold, in his arms.

"Who could have done this to him?" Laura sobbed, looking at Peter over Coffin's shoulder.

Peter twisted his head from side to side, moaning. With both hands he reached for his neck, and his fingers began exploring the wound, digging deep into the scarlet flesh.

"No, don't do that," Coffin said, grabbing the boy's wrists and pulling his hands away from his throat.

Peter's eyes suddenly focused on Coffin, and he lunged for Coffin's neck, his teeth snapping shut, just out of reach. Coffin leapt back, letting go of the boy's thin wrists.

Peter snarled, and snapped at Coffin again, like a wild animal. There was a red splodge on the sofa cushion, and Coffin realised that the boy had a nasty wound to the back of his head. Before Peter could leap off the settee, Coffin pinned the boy back down again, taking care to stay out of reach of the wildly snapping jaws.

"What's happening?" Laura said. "I don't understand why he's trying to bite you."

"Un, un, unnn," Peter moaned, and clicked his teeth together again, flecks of bloody spit flying from his mouth.

"Peter, shh, it's okay, it's okay," Coffin said.

"Un, nnn, nnii, unnn," Peter moaned again.

"Peter, where's Jacob?" Coffin whispered. "Where have you been, Peter? Where's Jacob, can you tell us?"

Peter whipped his head around, leaving clots of blood on the upholstery. "Nnniii, unnniiinnu, nniiiiiiinnuuuh."

"Oh, please!" Laura cried. "Where's my boy, tell us where my boy is!"

"Nnnniiiinnnnuuuuuuuu, nniiiiiinnnuh!"

"Nine," Coffin said. "Is that what he's saying? Nine?"

"Nine?" Laura cried. "What does that mean, nine? Why does he keep saying that?"

"Niiinnntuuuu, nnniiiiiinnntuuu, unnniiiiinnnnuuuh . . ."

"What is it, Peter," Coffin said, leaning in close. "What is it, what are you trying to tell me?"

The boy snapped at Coffin again, his teeth clicking together over and over, as he thrashed his head back and forth in a frenzy. Coffin jumped back out of the way, letting go of Peter's wrists. The boy leapt up, suddenly galvanised with a burst of energy, and crouched on the settee, like an animal.

Coffin stood in front of Laura, saying, "Get out, Laura. The kid's gone crazy, he's trying to kill us. Look at his eyes, he's lost it."

Laura backed up towards the door, keeping her eyes fixed on the bloodthirsty creature that had invaded her home.

Peter leapt off the settee, screaming as he hurtled at Coffin, arms reaching out, clawed fingers ready to latch onto him. He smacked into Coffin, who rolled backwards, and threw the child off, using his own momentum to send him tumbling across the room.

Laura, standing in the doorway, screamed, as the creature that had once been her son's friend, scrambled to its feet and snarled. Coffin jumped up, facing the child, and wiped blood off his face. It was Peter's blood, the blisters bursting, the skin sloughing off his face and hands.

Coffin noticed the boy's fingernails, some of them were hanging off, attached to his fingers only by raw tendrils of flesh.

What was happening to him? He looked like he was disintegrating in front of them.

The boy leapt at Coffin again, but this time there was no power behind it. Whatever demonic strength the boy once had seemed to be quickly evaporating. He landed at Coffin's feet, and Coffin saw the back of his head for the first time.

The skull looked like it had been flattened, beneath a tangled mess of hair and blood. Like he'd fallen, or been slammed against a wall. He crawled towards Coffin, grunting and moaning, his teeth snapping at Coffin's feet.

Stepping out of the way, Coffin watched as a bloody tooth dropped from Peter's mouth, and another, and another.

Coffin joined Laura by the door, placing an arm around her shoulders. A siren sounded in the distance.

"The paramedics will look after him," Coffin said. "They'll take him to hospital, they'll find out what's wrong with him."

Laura shook her head, crying, as they watched the boy squirming on the floor, moaning.

"Is this what's happened to Jacob?" she said. "Where is he, Joe? Where's my boy?"

"He kept saying nine, ninetuh. What does that mean? Nine, ninetuh."

The siren grew in volume, the ambulance pulling into Laura's street. Coffin looked out of the window. There was a police car behind the ambulance.

The last thing Coffin wanted right now was an encounter with the police.

"Laura, I've got to go, the police are here," Coffin said.

Laura looked up at Coffin, her tear stained eyes suddenly round with comprehension. "Ninety-nine!"

"What?"

"Peter, he was trying to say the number ninety-nine! I know he was."

The ambulance pulled onto the drive. The police were right behind it.

Coffin headed for the kitchen, at the back of the house, Laura following him.

"What's that got to do with anything, Laura?"

"No. 99 Forde Road! You remember, don't you, Joe?"

Coffin paused. Sure, he remembered.

"We had a call, a child, injured?" The paramedic stood in the front doorway, holding a kit by his side.

"Oh thank God!" Laura said, and pointed to the living room. "He's in there, please hurry!"

Laura herded Coffin into the kitchen and to the back door. "It's not locked. No. 99, Jacob's there, I know he is. He was fascinated by the place, I told him not to go snooping around, but he's there."

Coffin squeezed Laura's hand. "I'll find him."

He opened the door and sprinted across the garden. He stopped by the side of the house, and waited. Once he heard both of the police inside the house, he ran.

joe coffin
removes his sock

The car skidded as Tom braked, gravel shooting out from beneath the tyres, hitting the chassis like gunshots. Whatever he had hit last night had bent the driver's side door out of alignment, and jammed it shut. Forgetting that he'd had to climb through from the passenger side when he got in the car, he kicked and pulled at the door, screaming in frustration.

Remembering it was jammed shut, Tom scrambled over the handbrake and passenger seat, opening the door and falling on his face onto the gravel drive. He ran up to the front door.

Locked.

Fuck!

How long before that kid Peter told Coffin where he'd been kept prisoner?

If Coffin comes here, and finds Steffanie, if he sees the creature she's become . . . oh fucking shit.

Why the fuck did they leave Peter to wander around the house like their fucking pet mascot?

Tom ran down the steps, almost tripping and landing on his face again. He dashed around the back of the house. He'd forgotten to bring the key with him, but he had to get inside. If he had to break in, he would. They liked to stay out of the daylight, he knew that much. Probably upstairs in the bedroom, fucking each other's brains out, like a pair of fucking animals.

Using his elbow, Tom punched a pane of glass out, in the rear door. He reached through and found the key, still in the lock. He fumbled with it, his fingers shaking, until he got the door open.

He stumbled inside, hands against the walls to steady himself. Abel and Steffanie had to get out of here, before Coffin arrived. Perhaps Tom could persuade them to leave Jacob behind, if he was still alive. As much as Tom hated that fucking kid, the memory of him lying in that chair, looking like death, had been gnawing at him ever since.

"Hey!" he yelled. "Wakey, wakey, the fucking cavalry's on the way!"

Nothing, not a sound. Where would they keep Jacob? Tom ran down the stone flagged passage, into the gloomy reception hall.

Oh shit! What about the old guy, looks like something out of a fucking horror movie? How are we going to get him out?

Tom looked in the large living room, his eyes slowly adjusting to the poor light. No one, not even Boris Karloff sitting in the corner, waiting for his next feed.

Tom took the stairs two at a time.

At the top, Abel appeared out of the shadows, bringing Tom up short, with a little squeal of fright.

"Fucking hell!" he hissed. "Do you have to do that? I think I just lost another year of my life right then."

"Why are you here?" Abel said.

"It's Coffin, he's on his way." Tom cocked his head, sure he'd heard footsteps crunching on the gravel drive. "If he finds you here, you're fucking dead meat."

Abel put a hand to his mouth and giggled. The sound had a voluptuous, filthy quality to it, which made Tom nauseous for a moment.

"But I'm already dead," Abel said.

"Yeah, whatever," Tom said, backing up. "But if Coffin finds you, you'll be deader than fucking dead. Look, I haven't got time for this shit. Where's the kid?"

Abel advanced upon Tom, who was backing up to the stairs. "If our secret comes out, you will pay. You must hide Steffanie, and the Father."

"Hey no way, you're on your own now. I've been telling you to lie low, but because you couldn't keep your cock in your pants, everything's fucked up."

Tom stopped walking, his heels on the edge of the top step.

"You will take them, and you will hide them," Abel said. "I will deal with Coffin."

"Right, great. Just where exactly am I going to hide them, a fucking Travelodge on the motorway? I got news for you, Count Duckula, but the nearest you're going to get to a meal of blood in one of those places, is if they serve black pudding for breakfast."

Abel grabbed Tom by the throat, and pushed. Tom's arms windmilled as he was forced out over the stairs, his feet struggling to keep contact with the top step.

"You will do as I say, Tom Mills. We have a bargain. I will deal with Coffin, you will get Steffanie and the Father to safety."

"Okay!" Tom said, his voice a strangled whisper.

Abel pulled Tom back to safety and let go of his throat. Tom sucked in a hoarse breath, and took a moment to straighten his clothes. He walked backwards down the stairs a couple of steps, keeping his eyes on Abel the whole time.

"Fucking maniac," he muttered.

Tom found Steffanie in the kitchen. She had her head tipped back, and was holding one of the empty blood bags over her open mouth, squeezing out the last drips of blood. She looked at Tom, and smiled, blood dripping down her chin and neck.

The decrepit, old man sat at the table, blood smeared around his thin, cracked lips. He still looked dead to Tom.

"We've got to go, your husband's on his way, and as much as I'd like to say he'll be delighted to see you up and about, I don't think it would last."

"Do we really have to go right now?" Steffanie pouted. "I was having so much fun here."

"Yeah, well, the party's over for now. We've got to move, and Ebenezer Scrooge needs to come with us." Tom looked doubtfully at the old man. "I don't suppose you've got a wheelchair, have you?"

Steffanie folded her arms and stared at Tom. "I'm not going. We're safe here, this place is ours."

"Not anymore, it isn't," Tom shouted. "Are you listening to me? Coffin might not bring the filth with him, as they're not exactly on the best of terms with each other, but sooner or later, this place is going to be crawling with coppers, paramedics, reporters, who knows, maybe the fucking girl guides will have a look in too."

"He's right," Abel said, entering the kitchen. "You have to go."

Tom ran his hands through his short hair. He felt like his eyes must be bugging out of their sockets, on stalks like in the old Tom and Jerry cartoons.

Abel was naked.

"What the fuck, man!" he yelled. "Put some fucking clothes on, this isn't the time for playing hide the fucking sausage!"

Abel smiled, revealing his pointed teeth. He lifted a hand, holding out one finger, and ran the sharp fingernail across his chest, drawing a line of blood in its wake. Dipping his fingertip in the blood welling out of the cut, he drew red lines across his cheeks and over his nose.

"I'm preparing for battle," he said.

* * *

Emma sat in her car, across the road, and watched Tom hustling from around the back of the house, guiding a woman along beside him, a sheet over her head and shoulders. He looked drawn and pale, anxious. No, not anxious, he looked terrified. He kept casting glances all around as they moved, and Emma put her head down when he looked her way, convinced he had seen her.

But when she looked back up, he had his rear car door open, and was guiding the hooded woman inside, a hand on her head, so she didn't bump it. Emma thought he was going to climb in the car and reverse out of the drive, and she got ready to bow her head again, hide her face as he drove past. But he didn't. He shut the door on the woman, who stayed under wraps beneath the sheet, and ran back round the back of the house.

Emma watched the woman in the car, as spots of rain appeared on her window. The woman sat perfectly still in the back seat. She made no movement to take the sheet off. Why was that? Either she was hideously ugly, incredibly famous, an internationally hunted murderer, or just plain eccentric. But really, why was she so scared that she might be recognised?

Tom appeared from around the back of the house again, this time carrying a hunched figure beneath another sheet. Whoever this person was, they obviously weighed very little, as Tom had no trouble carrying them. A child maybe?

Tom opened the rear door of the car and slid the shrouded figure inside. He slammed the door shut, and this time he climbed in the car, through the passenger seat and over the handbrake into the driver's side. Emma heard the engine start up, saw the cloud of fumes spurt from the exhaust pipe.

She slid down in her seat, head bowed. She heard the car reverse onto the road, and then accelerate away. Sitting back up again, Emma caught sight of Tom's car as it paused at a junction, and then disappeared from view.

She debated following him, and decided against it. Her curiosity had been piqued by the house, and what it might contain. Tom Mills had certainly wasted no time driving down here. Emma had found it difficult to keep a tail on him at times, knowing that she would have stood out if she had driven as fast and recklessly as he had. Something had impelled Tom to rush over here, and Emma was longing to find out what.

Emma stepped out of her warm, dry car. The wind pulled at her hair, ruffled her jacket. Spots of rain fell on her face. She walked cautiously up the drive, examining the house's eccentric frontage for any signs of a break-in. How long, she wondered, had those two people been living in there? And what did Tom have to do with them?

Some of the windows on the front had been boarded up a long time ago, whilst others still had their original Victorian windowpanes. The ivy covering the house rustled in the wind, giving the building an appearance of life and movement.

Emma shivered.

No. 99 had been empty for as long as everyone could remember. There was an air of mystery about it, and many people, not just the local children, were convinced it was haunted. Once, a few years back, she had made an attempt to look into the house's history, and to find its current owner. But there was very little to go on. The paper trail was confusing and filled with gaps, and all Emma could find out in the end was that it was owned by a private individual, and it had been in their family for many years.

The reporter walked slowly along the front of the house, and followed the route around to the rear that she had seen Tom take. Branches rustled in the wind above her. There were tyre tracks in the long, wet grass at the back of the house. Tom hadn't driven in this far just now. Did that mean he'd been here before?

Emma stopped walking. A door at the back was wide open. Inviting her to step inside.

This was too much temptation to resist. Emma stepped through the doorway, and into a passage. The house smelt of damp. On her right was an open cellar door. Emma peered down the stone steps, disappearing into darkness. She looked for a light switch on the wall, but there wasn't one. Perhaps the house had been empty for so long, electricity had never been installed.

There were candles and matches at the top of the cellar, but Emma decided to move on. She had no desire to explore a dark cellar alone, with nothing but a candle to light her way. Emma had seen enough horror movies to know that was a bad idea.

She continued walking down the passage, past the kitchen and into the reception hall. Heavy drapes had been hung over the windows which weren't boarded up. It was difficult to see anything in the poor light. Emma walked across the reception hall, and into the living room.

Again, in here, the windows were covered with heavy drapes. Emma pulled at the drapes, trying to drag them open, until she grew impatient and yanked them down. The curtain poles ripped from the plaster, and clattered to the floor, clouds of dust billowing outward, like an explosion.

Emma waved the dust away, coughing. The light was still poor, but she could see better now. More layers of dust covered the heavy furniture, but even from across the other side of the room she could see the footprints in the dust, and the partially burned candles.

Somebody had spent time here recently. The same people that Tom had driven away with?

Emma walked deeper into the room.

She stopped walking by the fireplace. The dust was disturbed around the hearth, and the dust sheets had been removed from two of the chairs.

And there, on the floor, was a large patch of blood. Emma squatted, and pressed her hand into the carpet. The carpet made a squishing noise, little pools of blood growing around her fingertips, in the hollows created by the pressure of her hand.

The blood was cold and sticky, and there had obviously been a lot of it.

Emma stood up, and walked over to the living room door, rubbing the blood between her thumb and fingers. Floorboards creaked beneath her shoes, and she caught sight of her reflection in the mottled mirror as she passed it.

Emma stepped back into the hallway. She looked at the stairs, leading up to a landing. She could hear the traffic rumbling past at the front of the house. A thought struck her. She hadn't considered the possibility that Tom might be returning, after he had taken his passengers wherever they were going. She needed to get a move on, get out of the house and away, before he returned.

She decided to have a quick look around on the first floor, and then leave.

Emma headed for the stairs. She was halfway up the staircase when she heard the creak of a floorboard, the whoosh of air, just a moment before something slammed into her, knocking the breath from her body, and sending her tumbling down the stairs. She cracked her head against a step, and rolled over onto her shoulder, twisting her arm behind her back at an awkward, painful angle.

Stunned, she lay face down on the floor, struggling to breathe. Her lungs refused to obey her desperate need for air, as she fought for breath. Hands grabbed her by the hair and pulled her over, onto her back. The pain in her scalp made her scream, and suddenly she was breathing again, her chest heaving with the effort.

The face of a demon filled her field of vision. Black eyes stared at her from a face painted with streaks of blood.

"What a surprise," he whispered, as he leaned in close and began sniffing Emma's hair. "I wasn't expecting this."

Emma twisted her head away, as he buried his nose in her hair, making snuffling noises. He was on top of her, had her arms pinned to the floor by her sides. She screwed her face up as she felt his tongue sliding down her neck, his cold breath on her skin.

"Get the fuck off me!" she hissed.

He looked at her, his tongue snaking out of his mouth, licking his lips, running across the edges of his sharp teeth. Emma thought he looked very pleased with himself.

She snapped her head forward, her forehead connecting with his nose. The impact of his nose on her skull sent a sharp spike of pain through her head, but the man jerked back, loosening his grip on her arms. Emma scrambled backwards like a crab from underneath his body. Her attacker straightened up, squatting on the floor, grinning at her like an imp from Hell.

Emma's insides contracted at the sight of the man, his naked body smeared with bloody patterns, of lines and circles and crosses. His swollen cock was huge, and stiff, and he giggled when he saw her looking at it.

"Let's have some fun, shall we?" he said.

* * *

As he pounded down the street, bulldozing through shoppers, Coffin made a promise to himself that, first chance he got he would go back home and retrieve his Harley Davidson from the garage. He was wasting valuable time going everywhere on foot. Laura knew not to tell the police what was going on, she'd been a member of the Mob long enough for that, but still, this was different. This involved her son. For all Coffin knew, she might have blabbed to the coppers as soon as he left the house.

For all he knew there could be a cop car parked outside No. 99 right now.

When he turned onto Forde Road, Coffin slowed down, took his time looking up and down the street, checking for any signs of excitement. Nothing seemed out of the ordinary, just another boring, grey day.

Coffin knew the house he was looking for, remembered it from when he was a kid. Remembered breaking in there one time, and Tom squawking like a baby. Remembered thinking, *it's just a house, why are you crying?*

He could see its roofline now, the ivy crawling all over it, the distinctive shape of the Victorian build. Seemed like most of the original buildings surrounding it had been torn down, when the entire city went through a massive redevelopment during the 70s and 80s. But not this house, for some reason.

Amongst its bland, identikit neighbours, No. 99 looked like a ruined relic, saved from destruction through some obscure legal protection, perhaps. Whatever the reason, it had been standing empty for longer than anyone could remember.

Coffin approached the drive, alert for any sign of police. The drive was empty, the house dark. But somebody had been here recently. Through the growth of weed on the drive ran two parallel lines.

Car tyres.

Although the car was gone, that didn't mean to say the house was empty. Coffin ran through the options. Whoever had been holding Peter and Jacob prisoner might have made their escape, with or without Jacob.

Or somebody might still be in there, not realising that Peter had escaped. It seemed unlikely, as did the thought that a child kidnapper would hang around once they realised they had an escapee, who would probably lead the police back here.

It seemed reasonable to Coffin that the house was most likely deserted.

But that didn't mean he was going in there unprepared.

Coffin searched the overgrown borders, rooting through the weeds until he found a rock, slightly smaller than a grapefruit. He sat down between the two gargoyles and removed his shoe and sock. He put the shoe back on, and shoved the rock inside the sock, and swung it in a tight circle, smacking the rock into his open palm.

Coffin stood up and walked past the two gargoyles and up the steps to the front door. He twisted the handle and pushed and pulled at the door a few times. It stayed firmly shut.

Coffin walked back down past the sneering gargoyles and round to the rear of the house.

How had he got inside when he was a kid? There had been a gang of them. What had they done?

Now he remembered. That stocky, pimply kid, liked to think he was cock of the school, what was his name? Max, yeah, he'd smashed a window pane in the patio windows, reached through and unlocked the patio door.

Thought he was smart, but he wasn't. He cut himself reaching through that small windowpane, got Tom to give him his handkerchief, wrap his hand up.

Coffin would have let him bleed to death.

Round the back of the house he found an open door. That was too easy, almost like an invitation. But an invitation to what?

Coffin approached the door, slowly, gripping the improvised cosh in his fist. He walked through the back door, pausing in the stone flagged passageway. He could hear movement, scuffling.

The sounds of a struggle?

Coffin started running. He charged into the reception hall. A naked man, his sinewy flesh painted in streaks of blood, was on top of a woman, ripping at her clothes as she kicked and struggled beneath him. With a loud, guttural roar, Coffin charged at them, swinging the cosh high. The man looked up, eyes widening as he saw it hurtling towards him.

The rock smashed into his face with a loud crunch, and the naked man toppled back, off the woman. He landed face down on the floor, and was still.

Coffin looked at the woman, who was straightening her shredded clothes.

"Are you all right?"

"Yes, I'm okay," she said, getting shakily to her feet.

Her eyes widened, and Coffin began turning, just as the man slammed into Coffin, and sank his teeth into his shoulder. Coffin roared, as white hot pain shot through the muscle. He tried to shrug the man off, and his stomach rolled over as he felt teeth grating against his shoulder joint. With his free hand he punched his attacker in the face, once, twice, but still he would not unlock his jaws. Coffin swung around and smashed the man into a wall. The teeth came free, and he sank to the floor.

Coffin stepped away, as the man sprang into a crouch, and, snarling, leapt at Coffin, jaws wide open. Coffin smashed onto the floor, on his back, and his cosh went flying from his hand, skittering across the floorboards.

He grabbed his attacker's head, one hand either side of his face, as he lunged for Coffin's neck, jaws frantically snapping open and shut. Coffin had to strain to keep him from sinking his teeth into his flesh, he couldn't believe how strong this man was. Suddenly he stopped biting, and grinned at Coffin, exposing his white, pointed teeth against his blood painted face. Some of those teeth were broken, and his nose was little more than a bloody pulp. His black pupils filled his eyes, so that it seemed as though his eye sockets were empty, black orbs of infinity set above his high cheekbones dripping blood.

Suddenly he swiped his sharp, talon like fingernails across Coffin's cheek, a spray of blood arcing across the man's face. Coffin kicked him off, and rolled out of the way, cursing as his shoulder erupted with shooting pain. Coffin thudded into a wall, put his left hand on the floor to leverage himself up, and clenched his jaws as he realised he was too late.

The naked man slammed into Coffin, snarling, swiping sharp talons across Coffin's face again. He whipped his head back, but it was too late, and blood sprayed up the wall, and in his eyes.

Blindly, Coffin swung a fist, and it connected with the man's throat, forced him staggering back, clutching at his neck. Coffin wiped blood out of his eyes. He took advantage of the pause, and scrambled to his feet. Pivoting on his left foot, he swung his right up through a long arc, and into the man's skull, the heel of his boot squishing into his ruined face.

Coffin's attacker collapsed, all his fury and manic energy suddenly leaving him. He huddled on the floor, revolting in his blood streaked nakedness, his hands to his face, weeping. Walking in a circle around the pathetic creature, Coffin kept his eyes on him all the time. The best thing now would be to kick him in the head, cave in his face, and leave him there while he looked for Jacob.

"I can't fucking believe it."

Coffin spun round. He'd forgotten about the woman.

"What?"

"You beat him. I didn't think you could do it, but you did. You beat the fucking crap out of him."

Coffin wiped more blood out of his eyes. His face felt like it was on fire. "Why are you still here?"

"What, and miss the fight? Are you crazy?"

Coffin held up his hand for silence. The muffled sounds of crying behind him had changed. What was he doing now?

Was he giggling?

The thing on the floor uncurled itself and leaped at Coffin, the impact throwing him across the hall and smashing into a draped window. The glass shattered, and the heavy drape collapsed over the two men. Coffin punched out wildly, trapped beneath the cloth. Although his fists wouldn't connect with anything, he could feel the man slicing at him with his talons.

The flesh on his chest, and arms, and face, was being ripped open. Warm blood dripped into his eyes, the taste of it in his mouth. He couldn't breathe under here, had no freedom to fight.

Suddenly his fist connected with soft, yielding flesh, and he drove the punch home as forcefully as he could, piling all his weight behind it. He heard the crazed man hit the floor, and Coffin grabbed a handful of the dusty material and dragged it off him.

Pale daylight filled the hall, lighting up motes of dust whirling around in the air like mini hurricanes. Coffin threw the heavy drapes to one side, and blinked blood out of his eyes. He flexed the fingers in his right hand, pins and needles electrifying it. The lacerated muscle and tendons in his shoulder were slowing him down.

The man on the floor looked like an animal. He was crouching, lips peeled back in a snarl, black eyes staring at Coffin. Some of his flesh along his back, and down his right arm and thigh, was growing scaly and red where the sun was shining on it. As Coffin watched, the skin began blistering.

The creature didn't seem to notice. He drew himself up to his full height, smiling again.

"Where's the boy?" Coffin snarled. "What have you done with him?"

The man licked blood from his lips, and then ran at Coffin. Before he had chance to fully step out of the way, Coffin was overcome. The thing was on top of him, jaws snapping at his neck, a thin whining coming from deep in its throat.

Coffin tried to grab hold of him, his wrists, his arms, his neck, but his hands kept slipping off the blood smeared flesh. They staggered back like one life form, all whirling, struggling limbs, until Coffin snagged a foot under a rug and they both fell, hit the floor with a solid thump.

The thing sank its teeth into Coffin's right forearm, and he roared in pain. They seemed to go so deep, those teeth, into the muscle, scraping along the bone, chewing and gouging, tearing up the flesh and sinew.

Coffin pounded at the savage thing's head and back, with his fist, trying to break its grip. Crazed with bloodlust, the man let go of Coffin's arm and lunged for his neck. The long, pointed teeth scraped at his flesh.

He saw the woman, standing over them both, and she was raising her hand. What was she doing?

She was holding something, and it came swinging down, and Coffin suddenly realised it was his cosh, smashing into the man's head. The force of the blow whipped him sideways, and he rolled across the floor. As Coffin struggled to his feet, he saw the woman swing the cosh in a wide, powerful arc again, onto the man's skull.

Coffin heard bone crunch, saw blood and fragments of bone shower the woman's shredded suit. He glanced at his forearm. It was a mangled mess of blood and chewed tissue.

Coffin heard movement, looked up and saw the thing climbing to its feet again. It grabbed the woman by her hair. She screamed, grabbing at the man's wrists. Before Coffin could move, the man had smashed the woman's head against a wall, and let her go, to drop to the floor, senseless.

The rabid monster launched itself at Coffin again. They crashed through a door and rolled down the stone flagged passage. As they fought, they smacked against the walls, leaving trails of blood along the stonework.

Coffin struggled beneath the furious onslaught of the wild man. He scratched and bit and kicked at Coffin, like a rabid animal. Coffin's right arm was almost useless, and he used it little more than a shield held over his face. His chest, shoulders, arms and head were covered in lacerations, and blood sprayed against the walls as they fought.

Coffin managed to smash his elbow into the man's already ruined face, stunning him for a moment. Taking advantage of the pause, Coffin grabbed the man between his legs, and squeezed his balls tight. The naked man yowled in pain. Knowing he had to act fast, Coffin planted his left hand over the man's face, and smashed his skull against the wall. His black eyes widened in surprise, and Coffin pulled him forward and smashed his head against the wall again.

There was a crunch, something popped, and when Coffin pulled the man forward, he left behind a red splodge of hair and bone, and brain.

One more time, Coffin smashed the man's skull against the wall. There was another sickening crunch, and Coffin let him go. He slid down the wall, his head leaving a dark trail of bone and brain matter on the rough stone.

Coffin stepped away, keeping his eyes on the man's naked form all the time. He still expected him to jump up, snarling and hissing, teeth snapping, eyes rolling.

But no, he stayed still, back against the wall, head slumped on his chest.

Coffin wiped blood out of his eyes. His chest heaved with the exertion of the fight. He was covered in long, bloody lacerations, his shirt and trousers ripped, liked he'd been in a fight with a roll of barbed wire. He looked at the wound on his forearm, and tried flexing his hand. Pain rode up his arm and through his shoulder, but he could still move his fingers, rotate his hand.

There was an open door beside Coffin, steps leading down into a cellar. On a ledge at the top was a fat, church candle, and a box of matches. Coffin lit the candle, and walked down the steps.

He saw Jacob right away. The boy was lying on a makeshift bed of pallets and sacks, his eyes closed. From where Coffin stood, the boy looked dead. He approached him, holding the candle up to see him better. Hot wax dripped over Coffin's fingers, but he didn't notice.

Jacob's right arm was wrapped in a blood stained bandage. His face was drawn and pale, smudged with dirt. He stank of filth, and piss.

Coffin put the candle down, and squatted down in front of Jacob. The boy's chest was rising and falling in a slight, shallow movement.

Coffin snapped his head round as he heard movement upstairs. What would it take to kill that thing?

Coffin noticed the mantrap, its rusty jaws snapped shut. If he could prise the jaws apart, and if it still worked, that might do the trick.

Coffin braced his right heel against one jaw, and gripped the other with his left hand. Slowly the jaws separated, grinding and complaining. He kept pushing with his foot, and pulling with his left hand, until the jaws were fully extended, and he heard a click.

Coffin let go, and the mantrap jaws stayed in place. It was primed.

Standing with Jacob behind him, and the mantrap on the floor in front, Coffin watched as the creature crept down the stairs, the light from the candle dancing over its naked flesh, its hunched body casting a long shadow on the wall behind.

It seemed less human than ever, muscles rippling beneath blood soaked flesh, its cock hanging obscenely like a fat slug between its legs.

It fixed its black eyes on Coffin. He braced himself, every muscled bunched up, tense and ready.

This was going to hurt.

With a loud snarl, the creature rushed at Coffin, mouth open, teeth ready to sink into his soft flesh.

Ignoring the searing pain in his right arm, Coffin grabbed the mantrap in both hands and swung it at the creature. The jaws snapped shut with a wet squelch around its neck, the rusty spikes embedded into its throat. It staggered beneath the weight of the mantrap, its hands gripping the rusty contraption, trying to pull it apart.

The weight of the mantrap pulled it back, and the creature toppled over, hitting the cellar floor on its back. After struggling for a few more moments, legs kicking out in spasmodic movements, it finally lay still.

Coffin turned back to Jacob. His eyes were open.

"Joe?"

His voice was weak, nothing more than a hoarse whisper.

"I'm here," Coffin said, crouching down beside him. "I'm getting you out of here, Jacob. You're safe now."

Jacob closed his eyes.

Coffin wrapped his good arm around the boy and picked him up. Jacob raised his hands, his arms trembling, and hugged Coffin, who held him tight.

"St . . . Stef . . ." Jacob whispered.

"Shh," Coffin said. "It's all right, we're getting out of here now, get you to a hospital, to your mother. You're safe now."

Jacob fell silent, his body limp in Coffin's arms.

Coffin climbed the cellar steps, walked through the house, cradling the boy to him, gently stroking the back of his head with his ruined hand.

Outside, the rain clouds had cleared, and the touch of the pale, autumn sunshine on his face and arms, was like soothing balm to his raw, bloody wounds.

Bonus
Read the Next
Two Chapters

tight little stitches
in a dead man's face

The long column of grey ash projecting from the cigarette butt clamped between Doctor Shaddock's lips finally disintegrated and scattered over the table. Shaddock squinted at it through the spiral of smoke drifting across his face. Then he swept his hand over the table, and brushed the ash onto the floor.

"Fuck it, isn't one of you bastards going to offer me a drink?" he snarled.

Craggs nodded at the bouncer standing by the door, his back against the wall. Wearing the black Angels tee, with the angel wings outlined in white spread across his chest, he looked like he spent every spare moment down the gym, benchpressing twice his bodyweight before breakfast. He glowered across the room at Shaddock, like he was thinking to himself, *go get your own fucking drink, what am I, your fucking maid?* He pulled himself off the wall, sauntered around behind the empty bar, and pulled a bottle of lager from the fridge. He walked across the dance floor, nice and slow, like he had all the time in the world, and put the bottle on the table.

Shaddock looked up at him, the cigarette still stuck in his mouth. "What the fuck do you think I'm going to do with that? Stick it in my mouth and prise the fucking top off with my fucking teeth?"

Craggs nodded at the bouncer again. He sighed, and ambled back across the dance floor, to the bar.

"You need to sort your boys out, Mortimer," Shaddock said. "Kids, these days, got no fucking respect for their elders. Ain't that right, Joe?"

Joe Coffin sat across the table from Shaddock. He held a towel to his face. The towel had once been white, but was now stained scarlet. Coffin had removed his shirt. His right shoulder was a mess of torn flesh and blood, and his right forearm looked like a Rottweiler had given it a good chewing. His arms and chest and back were covered in red slashes, some of them still dribbling blood.

"Fucking hell, Joe," Shaddock mumbled. "What the hell did you do, break into the zoo and try shagging a tiger?"

"Forget the questions, Doc," Craggs said. "Just sew him up."

Shaddock twisted in his seat, and stared at Craggs. "This man should be in a hospital. He's probably lost a lot of blood, and he'll need the services of a good plastic surgeon if he wants to minimise the scarring on his face. Then there's the damage to his shoulder and arm." He twisted round and stared at Coffin. "You still got any use in that arm, Joe?"

Coffin lifted his arm and winced. "It hurts, but, yeah, I can use it."

"Clench your fist for me."

Coffin clenched and unclenched his fist, wiggled his fingers, and rotated his hand.

Shaddock pulled the cigarette from his mouth and stubbed it out in an ashtray. "Well, that's looking hopeful, I suppose. As your doctor, I'd still recommend you go to fucking hospital."

"If I go to a hospital, I'll be arrested before they get me on the table," Coffin said.

The bouncer returned and dropped a bottle opener on the table.

"Bout fucking time," Shaddock growled.

He prised the bottle top off, lifted the bottle to his lips and took a long slug of the cold lager. He swiped the back of his hand across his lips, pulled a cigarette from the crumpled packet on the table, and lit up.

"All right, then," he said, the cigarette waggling up and down in his mouth as he spoke. He lifted a large, black bag onto the table, opened it up and began rummaging through it. He pulled out scissors, bandages, packets of drugs and syringes, and sutures.

Coffin noticed the doctor's hands were shaking.

"I can sew you up, Joe, but it ain't gonna look pretty. I'm no plastic surgeon, the best I can do with your face is close up those wounds with some tight little stitches, try and minimise the scarring."

"We should take him to a hospital," the bouncer said. "Get him some proper treatment."

Shaddock lifted the lager bottle to his mouth, and drained the rest in one go. He slammed the empty bottle back on the table and grinned up at the bouncer. "You know what? I like these little French lagers. Get these fuckers chilled just right, they go down a treat. Best time I ever had drinking one of these, I was getting a blow job off a black whore down in Bearwood.

She was sucking on my dick, and I was sucking on the bottle. What do you think about that? I got an idea, why don't I go get myself another one of these fancy French lagers, and you can suck my cock while I drink it?"

The bouncer stared back at him, his eyes flat, his face deadpan.

"Go get him another drink, Clevon," Craggs said.

"Clevon?" Shaddock barked out a sharp, hard laugh. "What the fuck kind of name is Clevon?"

"He shouldn't be doing no operation on Joe when he's drinking and smoking," Clevon said. "It ain't right."

Coffin watched with interest as Shaddock stood up. He was tall and thin, looked like a stiff breeze might blow him over. He towered over Clevon, but the bouncer looked like he weighed at least twice what Shaddock did. Doctor Frankie Shaddock had been the Slaughterhouse Mob's private GP for as long as Coffin had been a part of the gang. How old was he now? Sixty? Seventy?

As the years had passed, Coffin had noticed Shaddock growing thinner, and more stooped, his hands becoming increasingly shaky.

But he'd always been a cantankerous bastard.

"These are some high class bouncers you employ these days, Mortimer," Shaddock said. "They got medical degrees and everything, at least this one must have, him telling me how to do my job and all."

"Clevon, get the doctor his drink," Craggs snarled.

The bouncer turned his back on Shaddock and ambled across the nightclub to the bar.

"All right, then," Shaddock mumbled.

He walked around behind Coffin and bent down and peered at the wound on his shoulder, the cigarette still clamped between his lips. Coffin winced as the doctor pressed his fingers down on either side of the gash, and pulled the edges apart. He looked intently into the wound.

"Hmm, doesn't look too bad, I suppose. Whatever it was bit you, has done some damage, but I'll see what I can sew up. It's going to be sore for a good while, though."

"What about infection, Doc?" Coffin said.

Shaddock grunted. "It would help if you'd tell me what bit you."

"You wouldn't believe me," Coffin said.

"Try me."

"It was a man bit me."

"You're right," Shaddock said. "I don't fucking believe you. You look like you've been savaged by a wild animal."

"You didn't see him," Coffin said. "He was like a wild animal."

Clevon slammed the bottle of lager on the table with a loud bang, and pointed at the doctor. "Hey, shouldn't he at least have washed his fucking hands?"

Shaddock snarled and walked away from Coffin. "All right then, seen as the fucking sphincter graduate over here obviously knows better than I do, I'll leave you in his capable hands, and he can fucking well put Joe back together again."

Craggs stepped in front of Shaddock and placed his hands on his shoulders. "Hey, Frankie, what's got into you? You know we respect you, I wouldn't have called you over here unless I trusted you. Come on, don't be like this. Joe needs *you* to put him back together, ain't that right, Joe?"

"Sure," Coffin said, the towel still pressed against his cheek. "Come on, Doc, I'm bleeding all over the floor, here."

Shaddock lifted the lager bottle to his mouth and drained half of it in one go. He smacked his lips together, and said, "For you, Joe, I'll stay. But dickwipe needs to leave. I'm not doing anything until he's gone."

"Clevon, go help Kirstin check the stock," Craggs said.

Clevon glowered at Shaddock some more, then turned and left.

Shaddock began ripping packets open on the table.

"Fucking wash my fucking hands, who the fuck does he think he's fucking talking to?"

"You're right, Frankie, kids these days they've got no respect for their elders," Craggs said. "You and me, we were born at a time when society had values. We spoke out of line, we got a good pasting from the old man, right?"

Shaddock filled a syringe from an ampoule. "Damn right." He shoved the needle into Coffin's left shoulder. "Giving you a shot of antibiotics, Joe, and I'll give you a tetanus jab, too. Whoever or whatever bit you, no telling what germs they might be carrying around. The mouth's a filthy fucker, Joe, full of nasty shit. Then I'll give you a local anaesthetic, before I sew you up." He stepped back, and regarded Coffin's wounds. "I'm gonna have to give you a fair few shots of local, enough they might knock you out a bit."

"Forget that, Doc," Coffin growled. "I've got things to do today, I need to be sharp."

Shaddock filled another syringe with the tetanus shot. "All right then, you're the boss. But sewing you up's gonna hurt like a bastard."

Craggs handed Coffin a glass of whisky. Coffin swallowed the drink in one, and slammed the glass down on the table. "I already hurt. Hurting some more isn't going to make it any worse."

Shaddock gazed at Coffin's face, at the blood and the ripped flesh. "Fucking hell, Joe, one of these days you're going to get yourself killed. And then I'll be putting tight little stitches in a dead man's face, making you look nice and pretty for your funeral."

* * *

Emma Wylde held the ice pack to the back of her head, and gazed at her reflection in the bathroom mirror. It was just a shame that Halloween had already been and gone, as the battered face that stared back at her would have been perfect for trick or treating. Her bloodshot eyes were encircled by dark, heavy shadows, and there was an angry bruise across her forehead, from when she had delivered her Glaswegian Kiss. How the fuck she was going to explain this to Nick, she had no idea. Especially as they were supposed to be meeting for lunch in another ten minutes. She had already shoved her shredded clothes into a black plastic bag and, apart from the evidence on her face, and a few light scratches across her stomach and shoulders, there was nothing else to show for her misadventure at the house.

But that was more than enough.

Standing in her bra and knickers, she examined the scratches across her abdomen. They were shallow, had hardly bled at all, but still, Emma was worried about infection. She should go to a doctor, but then there would be questions, and Emma wasn't sure she actually had any answers.

Not ones that made sense, anyway.

Emma opened the cabinet, and rooted through the packets of paracetamol, creams, lotions and Nick's eye drops. She found a packet of antihistamines. Weren't they supposed to be good for infections? Or was that allergies?

"Oh, fuck it," she muttered, and split the silver foil open, and popped a tiny tablet in her mouth.

What she really needed was a course of antibiotics. Or maybe a tetanus jab.

Emma shuddered when she thought of the hideous creature in that house. It was difficult to think of him as being human, more like a crazed, rabid animal. Those teeth, and his eyes. If Emma had held any belief in the supernatural, she would have considered the possibility that he was possessed.

Whatever. She'd been lucky to escape with her life, that was for sure. If Joe Coffin hadn't turned up when he had, Emma was convinced she'd have been ripped to shreds. After he'd shoved his big cock in one or more of her orifices, first though.

Emma suddenly felt faint, and sat down on the edge of the bath. She dropped her head between her knees and took some slow, deep breaths.

"Come on, keep it together. You're the big, bad reporter, remember? You don't take no shit from anyone. Wylde by name, wild by nature."

Giggles burst out of Emma's stomach, which was busily turning over and threatening to regurgitate her breakfast. What was happening here? Was she suffering some kind of hysterical fit?

"Oh, shit," she whispered, and lunged for the toilet.

When she'd finished throwing up, she sat on the floor, grabbed a towel, and wiped the sheen of sweat off her face.

Emma reached out a trembling hand and picked up the ice pack, and pressed it against her scalp again. From a tentative finger exploration, Emma was convinced she had a lump the size of an ostrich egg on her head. She imagined it throbbing, and pulsating with a red glow, like in the old Loony Tunes cartoons. The last thing she remembered was being grabbed by the hair and dragged across the room.

From that point on it was one big blank, until she came to in the silence of the house. That might have been the scariest part of the whole ordeal, wondering where that monster was, if Coffin was still alive, and was she a prisoner, now?

As it turned out, it appeared she had simply been forgotten about. Coffin was nowhere to be seen. Emma had climbed painfully to her feet, holding onto the wall to steady herself. She had a piercing headache, which spiked down from the top of her skull to right behind her eyes. Her vision swam in and out of focus, and Emma had to stand by the wall, using it as support for a minute, before she felt well enough to walk unaided.

It was clear where the fight had happened. Emma followed the trail of blood to the passage leading to the back of the house and the kitchen. Huge, arcing sprays of blood decorated the damp, mildewed walls, like a Jackson Pollock painting.

Emma wondered whose blood it was.

She followed the trail to the top of the cellar steps. There was a splodge of blood and hair, and some other stuff she really didn't want to think about too much, on the wall there. But no sign of a body anywhere.

Emma stood at the top of the steps, peering down into the darkness.

Did she really want to go down there and investigate?

She had decided not.

Then she'd heard the police sirens, in the distance, but definitely growing louder.

Emma had got the hell out of that house as quickly as possible.

She shifted the ice pack slightly.

Joe Coffin.

Terry Wu's murderer, at least according to Steffanie.

But now Emma's rescuer.

Okay, so he pulled a rabid, possibly possessed schizoid with a boner the size of a donkey's dick off her, but where was he when she woke up? And why was he there in the first place? Did it have anything to do with Tom Mills and his mysterious companions?

The front door slammed shut downstairs.

"Hey, Emma?" Nick shouted.

Emma reached across the bathroom and shoved the door shut.

"I'm on the toilet!" she shouted.

I can't believe this. Earlier on this morning I was hiding in Tom Mills' bathroom, and now here I am, hiding in my own.

"Sorry, Ems, but I can't make our lunch date today," Nick shouted up the stairs. "I've just had a call to go into work, looks like those two missing kids have been found."

"That's great!" Emma shouted, and winced at a spike of pain lancing through her head.

"Yeah, it is, but the house where they were being kept? Apparently it's a bloodbath. I'll try and phone you later, let you know when I'm coming home."

"Okay."

Emma listened for the front door slamming shut again, and then breathed out.

A house that looked like a bloodbath? Was it the same house? Was that why Joe Coffin was there, looking for Jacob?

But what did Tom Mills have to do with any of this? Jacob was his kid. Surely he wouldn't have been keeping his own son a prisoner in an abandoned house with a violent madman?

Emma hauled herself upright, and gazed at her ruined face in the mirror again. Was there any possible chance that makeup might hide those bruises? Not that she had ever been a makeup kind of girl.

Deciding to forget about trying to hide her bruises with makeup, Emma opened the bathroom door and walked stiffly into her bedroom.

She dressed quickly and hurried downstairs, grabbed her bag and her laptop. As she headed for the front door, she saw the study door had been left open. She could see Nick's desk, and his chair, and she smiled as she remembered last night, how they had both managed to forget work for a short while at least.

And then another thought occurred to her.

The file he had been looking at.

Joe Coffin.

Emma put her bag and laptop down in the hall and walked into the study. The file was still lying on the desk, in front of the computer monitor.

She stood over it, looking at the manila cover, afraid to touch it. Would it be a betrayal of Nick's trust if she opened the file and looked inside? If he found out, he'd go crazy.

But if he never found out, what did it matter?

Without moving the folder from where it lay, Emma flipped open the cover. Now that she had time to examine it, she could see it wasn't an official police document.

What was going on? Did Nick have a personal vendetta going against Joe Coffin? Nick had been instrumental in getting Coffin prosecuted for the assault that sent him to jail, but with Craggs' lawyers involved, Coffin was sentenced to far less time than Nick had been hoping for.

Emma leafed through the folder. It was a catalogue of extortion, money laundering, drug supplies, and killings, that Coffin was suspected of having been involved in.

But with no evidence to support any of it.

At the front was a report on two young men who had been found murdered in their flat. The murders looked like an execution style killing. Nick had scrawled one name over it.

COFFIN?

maybe superman

Jacob Mills lay in the hospital bed, eyes closed, tubes snaking from his frail body, leading to drips and a heart monitor. His mother sat by the side of the bed, holding his hand, his arm heavily wrapped in bandages. She gently stroked his fingers with her thumb, her eyes fixed on his pale, drawn face.

Tom Mills, sitting on a stiff, plastic chair on the other side of the bed, felt like shit. He had to sit on his hands to stop from fidgeting, and he had to use every bit of willpower he could summon, to stop himself from leaping out of the chair and stalking up and down the hospital room. Pain flared through his chest every time he took a breath, and his head and neck felt like someone had pounded at him with a metal bar.

Fortunately for Tom, by the time the emergency staff had discharged him, the police had finished with their questions for Laura, and already gone. They'd be back, of course, but the longer Tom could keep out of their way, the better.

Tom hated hospitals. The smell of antiseptic, mixed with the stink of old, sick people, which seemed to be ever present in hospitals no matter what ward you were on, made him feel ill. The reek of sickness and death reminded him of his father, and his final days as the cancer ate away at his body. Tom hated that old bastard, and hated every moment spent looking after him while he took his time dying, but he wouldn't wish a death like that on anyone.

Well, maybe he could think of a few. But as for himself, he'd rather eat a bullet when the time came, than spend his final months on earth lying in a bed, pissing and shitting all over the sheets, and having his arse wiped by some gorilla who was too fucking stupid to get a proper job.

The kid, though, he hadn't deserved any of this. Poor little bastard shouldn't have gone exploring in that house. Bloody typical. That house was cursed, it had to be. No wonder it had drawn a maniac like Abel to it. Tom should have moved them on, first chance he got. There were always people breaking in to it, having a look round, or some homeless guy dossing down for the night.

But not Jacob. Why the hell did he have to go and choose now to take up a career in breaking and entering? Any other time, Tom might have been proud of him. It was that Peter Marsden's fault. If not for him, Jacob never would have dared break into that house. And then none of this mess would have happened.

Tom wondered what the doctors were making of Peter's condition. His wounds, in his throat and the back of his head, the blisters. And then there was the fact that he kept trying to take a bite out of anyone who got close enough. He was like a wild animal. No one was taking any chances, and they were keeping him sedated, and strapped in the bed, just to be on the safe side. He'd already bitten one nurse in the Emergency Room, and then made a grab for the bag of blood on his IV drip.

Even that miserable old bint that passed for his mother was keeping away from him.

At least Jacob wasn't in that condition. Whatever else they had done to him, they hadn't tried turning him into one of them.

Tom ran his fingers through his hair. Felt like the walls were closing in on him, like he was going to scream if he didn't get out of here soon.

"Hey," he whispered.

Laura dragged her eyes away from Jacob. Her face was lined and pale, dark shadows under her eyes from worry and lack of sleep. She stared mutely at Tom.

"I'm just going to go outside, smoke a fag. This place is killing me, I feel like I'm going crazy. I won't be long."

Laura said nothing, just turned and looked at Jacob again.

"You want anything from downstairs? I could get you a coffee, or something to eat?"

Laura shook her head.

Tom stood up, wiped his hands, clammy with sweat, down his trouser legs. Looking at Jacob, swamped in the big hospital bed, Tom wanted to cry. He had a sudden urge to tell Laura everything, spill his guts to her, to the police, just get it all off his chest and out in the open. Maybe that would be for the best. Confession was supposed to be good for the soul, right?

Tom walked out of the room, down past the nurse's station, and out onto the main corridor.

Tom stood in the car park and lit up a cigarette. The late afternoon light was slowly fading as the sun set behind the cloud cover. A long line of cars waited to get moving, queuing up to leave the car park. Someone sounded their horn, impatient to get moving.

A hand closed around Tom's upper arm, the grip strong, and Joe Coffin said, "Enjoying your cigarette, Tom?"

"Oh, hey, Joe, I—"

"Come with me," Coffin said, glancing around.

He began walking, guiding Tom out of the car park and past decorative bushes, into a corner of the hospital building where they were hidden from view.

Tom's eyes widened as he saw the blood stained dressings on Coffin's face, and over his hands. "Fuck, Joe! What the fuck happened to you?"

"Never mind that," Coffin hissed. He snatched the cigarette from Tom's mouth and threw it away. "What the hell's going on, Tom?"

"What? What are you talking about?"

Coffin leaned in close, towering over Tom. "Have you seen the state Jacob's in? Poor kid was being kept prisoner in a cellar by a maniac, looked like a fucking vampire. You know anything about this, Tom?"

"No, of course not," Tom said.

"Where the hell did you run off to?" Coffin snarled.

"It was seeing that Peter kid, staggering towards the house like a zombie. I just had a flash, like a premonition or something, and I knew where Jacob was. You found him at the house, right? The one we broke into as kids?"

"Yeah, that's right. Where the hell were you?"

"I was in such a panic, I just wanted to get to Jacob as fast as I could, you know, and I wasn't concentrating. I fucking totalled the car, Joe, lost control and skidded smack into a brick wall on the way over there. I was out, for like, ten minutes or more, and then the ambulance turned up, and they brought me here."

Coffin stared at Tom, his eyes narrowed, like he didn't believe him.

"I'm being fucking straight with you, Joe," he said. "My chest is black and blue from when the airbag hit me, look."

With trembling fingers, Tom unbuttoned the top of his shirt and pulled it open. His chest was a mass of bruises, just like he'd said.

"Where's your car now?" Coffin said.

"Fuck knows, I got taken away in an ambulance, I don't know, it's probably been towed away by now."

Coffin eased back a little, not so much in Tom's face anymore. "How's Jacob, you seen him yet?"

"Yeah, yeah, me and Laura, we've been sat by his bed all afternoon, you know. He's in a bad way, but the doctors are keeping him sedated for the moment. They say he's in shock, and he's lost a lot of blood."

"That maniac at the house, I think he might be the one who killed Steffanie and Michael," Coffin said.

"No, Joe, you got those guys, remember?"

Coffin got in Tom's face again, up close. "Those two punks? I don't know where you got your info from, but they probably couldn't have stolen sweets from a baby, never mind kill someone. No, that bastard at the house," Coffin pointed to the dressings on his face, "he did this to me, chewed me up like a slab of beef at the butchers, he's the one killed Steffanie and Michael, I know it."

"All right, Joe, whatever you say."

Coffin stuck his finger in Tom's face. "Yeah, that's right. Whatever I say."

"What happened to the other guy, Joe?"

Coffin stepped back again, relaxed a little. "I killed him."

"Good," Tom said. "The bastard deserved it."

"There was a woman there, too."

Tom stiffened up, felt his insides clenching. *Not Steffanie, she was with me.*

Coffin glanced behind him, at the cars in the car park, an ambulance, lights flashing, pulling into the Emergency Department entrance. He seemed on edge, wanting to keep out of sight.

"You all right, Joe?"

"Sure, everything's just dandy," Coffin hissed, snapping his head back around to stare at Tom. "Here I am, fresh out of prison less than forty-eight hours, and I've executed two drugged up, lowlife snotwipes, and killed a deranged psychopath. Now, there's probably a great many people might well want to line up to shake my hand for ridding the planet of three such dangerous degenerates, but the cops, nah, somehow I think they'll be taking a different view. So yeah, I'm on edge a little right now, as the hospital isn't the best place I could pick to hide out in."

Tom held up his hands, palm out. "All right, Joe. Fuck, I was just asking, is all."

"Yeah, well don't ask anymore. This woman, at the house, I'm pretty sure I've seen her before, parked outside your house earlier this afternoon."

"Ah, shit!" Tom said. "It's that reporter, the bitch has been sniffing around, asking questions, thinks she's Lois Lane, like she's onto some big story. I thought I'd got rid of her."

"How did she end up at the house on Forde Road?" Coffin said.

"Come on, Joe, how the fuck should I know? Maybe Superman flew over the house, saw what was happening with his X-Ray vision, and reported back to Lois!"

"Or maybe she tailed you to the house?"

"I already told you, I drove head on into a fucking brick wall on the way there!"

"What's her name?"

"I don't know, she never introduced herself. She works for the *Birmingham Herald*, I think."

A police car rolled past, pulling up in a waiting bay. Two policemen got out, and headed for the hospital main entrance.

"This place is getting too hot for me," Coffin said. "Stay with Laura and Jacob, and don't repeat anything I told you, okay? Especially not to the cops."

"Hey, I never would, Joe, you know that," Tom said.

With one more look around, Coffin set off at a fast paced walk across the car park. Tom watched him until he disappeared from view.

He let out a sigh of relief. That had been a close one. After hiding Steffanie and Rumpelstiltskin, Tom had come up with the excuse of rushing to the house, but crashing his car on the way. He'd known he had to make it convincing though, and that he had to actually crash his car.

The hardest part had been sitting behind the wheel, his seatbelt off, psyching himself up to drive full tilt into the wall he had picked. Trusting in the car's airbag system to stop him from taking a dive headfirst through the windscreen had been the hardest part.

Once he'd committed to the idea, he had floored the accelerator, only closing his eyes at the moment before impact.

It had worked like a dream.

Even though his chest and head hurt like a bastard, now.

Get
Joe Coffin
Free!

Yes, Free!
Joe Coffin Season One

If you enjoyed Joe Coffin Episode One, you might want to sign up to my **VIP** readers' list.

First up you will get the complete **JOE COFFIN SEASON ONE**, as a thank you for joining my list. No strings attached, you can even unsubscribe as soon as you have your book.

But you might not one want to, because next I will give you my collection of short stories **POPULATION:*DEAD!* AND OTHER TALES OF HORROR AND SUSPENSE**, featuring **HOW TO EAT A CAR** and **MRS DE RUNTZEN'S JEWELS**, both of which have been adapted for radio by Tall Tales and **THE MAN WHO MURDERED HIMSELF, DRIVE FAST SHE SAID** and the title tale **POPULATION:*DEAD!*** a horror/western mashup, plus more.

I'm not even going to mention your third book for joining my list, except to say it's a rock n roll, sex n drugs tale of faith and God, and it's called **SPEAKING IN TONGUES.**

WANT EVEN MORE?

YOU GOT THAT TOO!

Every week I send out an email with *giveaways and prizes*, including books by other authors who I think you will like too, plus updates on my work and *member only* books for sale which are not available anywhere else, including Amazon!

Sign up here:

www.kenpreston.co.uk

Other Books by Ken Preston

Joe Coffin Season One

Joe Coffin Season Two

Joe Coffin Season Three

Population:*DEAD!*
and Other Stories of Horror and Suspense

Speaking in Tongues

Young Adult
Planet of the Dinosaurs Book One: Project Wormhole

Caxton Tempest at the End of the World

Writing as M.J. Jackson
Twenty Seconds to Free Fall

Christmas in Paris

Lethal Injection

Hollywood Adventure

The Ocean's Slave

Printed in Great Britain
by Amazon